LOSING
Us

the SEX ON THE BEACH series

LOSING
Us

the SEX ON THE BEACH series

Jen McLaughlin

Copyright © 2015 by Jen McLaughlin

All rights reserved. No part of this book may be reproduced, transmitted, downloaded, distributed, stored in or introduced into any information storage and retrieval system, in any form of by any means, whether electronic or mechanical, without express permission of the author, except by a reviewer who may quote brief passages for review purposes, if done so constitutes a copyright violation.

This book is a work of fiction. Names, places, characters and events are fictitious in every regard. Any similarities to actual events and persons, living or dead, are purely coincidental. Any trademarks, service marks, product names, or named features are assumed to be the property of their respective owners and are used only for reference. There is no implied endorsement if any of these terms are used.

Manufactured in the United States of America Print ISBN: 978-0-9907819-3-6

Manufactured in the United States of America eBook ISBN: 978-0-9907819-2-9

The author acknowledges the copyrighted or trademarked status and trademark owners of all the wordmarks mentioned in this work of fiction.
Edited by: Kristin at Coat of Polish Edits

Copy edited by: Hollie Westring
Cover Designed by: Sarah Hansen at © OkayCreations.net
Interior Design and Formatting by: Tianne Samson with E.M. Tippetts Book Designs
emtippettsbookdesigns.com

E.M. TIPPETTS
BOOK DESIGNS

When it all comes crashing down...

Everything I thought I had with Austin Murphy—safety, stability, the normalcy I crave but my celebrity lifestyle rarely allows—was ripped away in one night. I wanted to surprise him, but the joke was on me. Now I don't know if I ever really knew him at all.

Someone has to pick up the pieces...

Mackenzie Forbes was everything I ever wanted and the one person I didn't deserve. When a past mistake costs me the girl I love, I'll do everything I can to get her back. We both have demanding careers and family secrets darkening our pasts, but I need Mackenzie in my future.

Sometimes everything you have to give just isn't enough...

To Greg. My love, my heart, my partner. I love you.

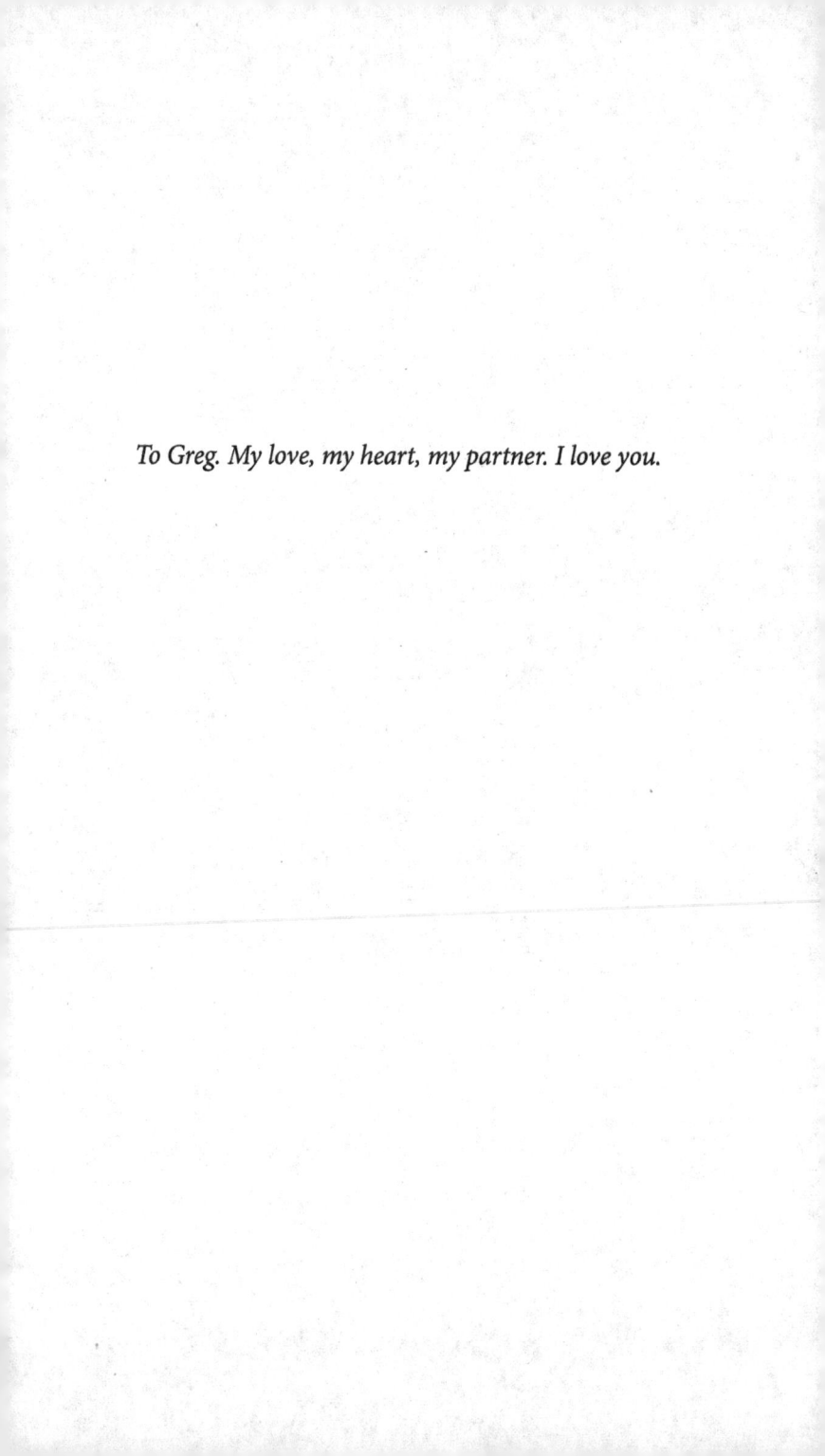

CHAPTER One

Mackenzie

Austin Murphy had a way of making a song seem more intimate than a night in between the sheets with him. And I'd been between the sheets with him enough times to speak from experience. I stood backstage, hidden behind a speaker since he didn't know I'd come back to Nashville yet, watching him sing with a racing heart.

It was the first thing I'd done when I met him, watching him sing, and I still couldn't stop watching when he performed. When he stepped up on the stage, the whole world stopped and stared. It was if time itself stood still and waited for him to finish. There was something about him, his looks or his voice or his charisma, that demanded as much. And the universe listened.

During the past few months, his career had really taken off. He'd opened for me over the summer for my world tour, and the buzz had initially been all "*Mackenzie Forbes's bad boy lover tours with America's Sweetheart*" but it had quickly turned into "*Austin Murphy, heartbreak extraordinaire, takes America by storm!*" instead.

No one had been happier about that than me.

After he'd finished his booking with me a little under three months ago, he'd gone back home, so Rachel could to return to school instead of studying remotely, but the buzz hadn't stopped. While Rachel had been working on advanced geometry and chemistry, Austin had been working his butt off in his studio in Miami. I hadn't seen him since.

It had been *months*.

The only reason he was doing this show was because he was in Nashville for one last concert with me, for the ending of my tour, but that wasn't for another two nights. Rachel was with Mrs. Greer, checking out a college, so she was fine back home. Plus, she was seventeen, so she was getting to be more independent. Austin had found a way to balance family and his dreams, and I couldn't be happier for him. Really.

But I missed him *so much*.

Our reunion was needed more than ever.

I was on the last leg of my North American tour, and then he was going to kick off his own in the summer. A whirlwind national tour that spanned all of America in three months, since that's all he could do because of Rachel's schooling. I'd be busy in the studio myself, working on my next album, so the chances of seeing him were slim to none. And if that didn't make matters worse...

There were rumors. Lots of them.

I, of course, knew better than to listen to them. But he'd been different lately on the phone. Distant, almost, and I had the sinking suspicion he wasn't happy. The tabloids were constantly showing off pictures of him with his arms around other women, beaming as if he'd died and gone to heaven down in Miami, surrounded by hordes of women dying to get in bed with him. Logically, I knew they were just the standard pictures you take with fans after a show, but some of them had looked like more.

And that scared me more than you'd ever know. I took a steady breath, watching as he finished his next-to-last song. Next would be the song he'd written for me. It was his way of saying he loved me, singing my song at the end of every show.

Smiling, I closed my eyes and waited.

He cleared his throat, waiting for the screams and the shouted *I love you*'s to die down. If so, he'd probably be waiting a long time. "Thank you, I love you too."

Opening my eyes, I willed him to turn his head and look at me, but he took his Redskins hat off and swiped a forearm across his forehead. I needed to see those bright blue eyes looking at me with love and warmth and—

"I normally close with the song I wrote for Mackenzie Forbes, as you all know, but tonight, I'm feeling a different song. One that'll be on my next album." He paused, letting the crowd go crazy. "You want to hear it early, before anyone else?"

They went wild, shouting and crying and screaming. The majority of the crowd was, of course, women. His lifestyle was so similar to mine, and yet so different at the same time. The majority of my fans were girls who wanted to be me, and the majority of his fans were also girls who wanted to be me— except it was because they wanted to screw him. I was simply the one who got to *do* so.

He strummed the guitar and stepped up to the mic, closing his eyes. I leaned in, breath held, needing to hear the song he'd replaced mine with.

You walked into the room,
All roses and sunshine.
I didn't know then, what I know now...
Thought you would never be mine.
But you are...
Oh, you are.

As he sang, tears filled my eyes but didn't spill out. He'd written me another song, and it was as beautiful as the last. At least, I assumed it was about me. If he was singing about another girl being his, well, then we had more problems than I'd thought.

Barely moving, I listened until he played the last chord, letting it drag out long and clear, then backed away from the speaker. I'd go wait for him in his dressing room and surprise him there with a kiss and maybe a few well-placed caresses. And then once we got home…

He would be *all* mine.

Any doubt I might have had about him, about *us*, faded away. I'd been a fool to doubt our love, and an even bigger fool to fall for the oldest trick in the book—the paparazzi's lies. Austin wouldn't cheat on me. He loved me, and I loved him. And that was the truth. In a week, we'd hit our one-year anniversary, which was why I was here early. It was time to reconnect and remember who we really were. Not the Austin Murphy and Mackenzie Forbes the world saw, but the real us.

It had been too long since we'd been just two people in love.

I'd blown off a few days in the studio, but I didn't care. I'd finished all my finals, I'd finished recording two songs, and now it was time for me to actually live. With *him*. After the show, we'd fly back to Florida. I was spending all of spring break there, because my best friends Quinn and Cassie were coming down too. We were having a reunion, of sorts. Cassie had to go down for a trial, and I lived there now—when I wasn't busy touring or recording songs—and Quinn had joined in, so we could all have our annual spring break trip. It had been too long since I'd seen them, and I couldn't wait.

Almost as much as I couldn't wait to surprise Austin in his dressing room.

I slipped inside the doorway and closed it, leaving the lights off. Once he came in and settled down, I'd slide up behind him, close my hands over his eyes, and whisper, "Guess who?" all seductively in his ear.

It was our little game we always did when we snuck up on one another. And he'd pull me onto his lap, our lips would meet, and everything would be okay. *Better* than okay, because we'd be together again. That's all we needed.

Lightning flashed outside his window, and I jumped. A big storm was coming, and I wanted nothing more than to get out of here before it hit, get tucked in under the blankets together, and wait it out the best way possible—naked, in each other's arms.

That's also all we needed.

The door opened, and the light flicked on. I hid behind the changing screen in the corner, a ridiculously big smile on my lips, and peeked around the corner. The smile quickly slid off my face, though, because it wasn't Austin…

It was some blonde chick I'd never seen.

She ripped off her shirt, and since she didn't have a bra on, it didn't leave much to the imagination. *At all.* And, damn, but the girl had big boobs with silver barbells through the nipples. She looked as if she had no doubt of her welcome in Austin's room. I had to wonder if she had reason to feel that way.

Just as I was about to step out and tell her to get the hell out of my boyfriend's room, the door opened and Austin strode in, whistling through his teeth. His dark ink swirled down his arms, as hot as the day I'd first met him, and his dark brown hair was barely visible under his hat. He wore a dark gray T-shirt with a dragon on it, tight black jeans, and a cocky grin. Underneath that grin was the chin dimple I loved so much, but instead of wanting to kiss it right now…I wanted to punch it. And him.

And the girl with the pierced boobs.

He closed the door behind him and stopped, his eyes on the blonde in his chair. Collapsing against the door, he locked it. Actually locked it, instead of turning around to leave. "You can't just…come in here like this, Diane. Put your shirt back on before someone comes in and sees you. Quickly."

"Why not?" The blonde pouted and stood up, sashaying over to Austin. When she reached him, she trailed her finger down his chest and over his abs, pausing above his waistband. Austin's jaw tensed, but he didn't move away. "You said it yourself the other night. You're lonely and confused and want more out of life than what you're getting with that sweet, wholesome country girl. I can give it to you, just like I said the other night. You didn't object then."

Austin caught her hand. "I was drunk that night, and I didn't mean any of the things I said, or might have done. None of that should've happened. We need to both pretend it didn't, and forget it all."

"I'll never forget any of it." She laughed. "Not in a million years. You wrote that new song for me, didn't you? Admit it."

He tugged on his hat. His nervous tic. "Look, I don't know—"

The girl didn't give him a chance to finish that sentence that I so desperately wanted to hear, because she planted those overly painted lips of hers right over my boyfriend's. He'd said he was lonely and wanted more than I could give him? And then he'd said that she should "pretend it never happened," and it didn't take much to figure out what he'd like to pretend hadn't happened.

How could he?

Tears blurred my vision, and I stepped out from behind the screen just in time to see him step back from the hussy who was apparently more his style than me.

He held her hands in both of his wrists. "*Diane.*"

"You want more than I can give you?" I asked at the same time, my voice low and steady, despite the way my heart had shattered the second that woman had walked into the room, and he hadn't sent her away. "That's what you want?"

"Shit," Diane said, her brown eyes wide.

Austin froze, his face pale as a ghost, his hands still on her wrists. "Mac. *No.* This isn't what it looks like."

He knew this girl, and he'd told her he didn't want to be

LOSING Us

with me anymore. I couldn't believe this was happening. Any of it. "Don't. Don't even waste your time trying to…to…make this okay. I heard, and saw, everything."

He dropped the blonde's wrists and stepped closer to me, hands outstretched. "Mac, *no*! You have to let me explain."

I stumbled back, tears running down my face. "Actually, I don't. I think I heard enough, thank you very much. I came here early to surprise you…" I shook my head and bit my lower lip, my hand closing on the knob and turning it. "But instead I'm the one who got the surprise. If you weren't happy, you could have just told me. You didn't have to…to…" I gestured to the blonde, who watched us with wide eyes—topped with artificial lashes. Bad ones, at that. "Cheat on me."

He hurried toward me, tripping over Diane's shirt, and almost fell flat on his face. "You have to believe me. I never—"

Unable to listen to another word, I shook my head and ran out into the cool Nashville evening air. I made it outside in record time, and for the first time, I thanked my personal trainer for being such a hard-ass when it came to my daily workouts. Because I needed to get away from the man I loved before he broke me even more than he already had. He'd done the one thing he'd sworn to me he'd never do.

He'd broken my heart.

CHAPTER Two

Austin

"Put your damn shirt on, and if you ever come near me again, I'll place a restraining order against you. We aren't, and never will be, together." I locked eyes on Diane, the woman who had started out as a friend and turned into a crazy stalker woman after the other night, and then apparently followed me to Nashville, of all fucking places. "Understood?"

Diane swallowed hard and nodded. "Yes."

Not wasting another second on her, I took off down the hallway of the backstage area. My heart pounding in my chest, I tore after Mac at full speed. I knew what she'd heard, and what she'd thought was happening, and I didn't blame her for thinking it. I mean, a woman had stripped down in my room and then spoken to me with familiarity—which was on *me*—and then kissed me as if she had a right to do so.

If the roles had been reversed, I'd have been pissed as hell too.

But, damn it, she had to give me a fucking chance to explain. Yes, I'd had a bad night where I'd had too much to drink and felt alone in the world—because I'd missed *her*. That was why I'd gotten drunk and opened my idiot mouth. But I loved her more than life itself, and I'd never, ever cheat on her.

When Diane had kissed me, I'd frozen, yes, but out of shock, not desire. Why would I ever want anyone else when I had Mac? I didn't. Couldn't.

Pushing through the doors, I sucked in a big breath, my head swimming because I was out of breath. Sprinting after your girl after doing a full show was not the best of ideas on a good day, but this obviously wasn't a good fucking day. Why, of all the days she could have come, did Mac pick the day that a chick decided to go all crazy on me and strip in my room? It's not like that was an everyday occurrence or anything.

Though I was starting to worry it might become one. It might be time to get security, like Mac had. Women could be crazy, man, when it came to singers.

I was learning this the hard way.

Bursting through the doors, I skidded onto the sidewalk. I saw her instantly. She waved to her driver frantically from the curb, motioning the black town car to come over to her. The man obeyed and pulled out into traffic, seconds away from reaching Mac's side and taking her away from me. I knew I had one chance to make her believe me. To show her I wanted her and only her…

And then she'd be gone for good.

I walked up behind her, taking a calming breath. I couldn't panic and act like a fool. "Mac, please. Let me explain."

She stiffened in front of me, her hands lifting and swiping at her cheeks. Knowing I'd done this to her, made her cry, sent a fist of pain punching through my chest. I wasn't supposed to make her cry—I was supposed to make her smile, damn it. I'd fucked up, and I'd fucked up big time. And now I had to make it right.

Somehow or another, I had to fix this.

Lightning flashed above us, followed by a loud boom of thunder. A storm was coming, and it was about to hit. We had to go to shelter before it did.

Together.

Turning slowly, she faced me. The pain in those bright green eyes echoed my own, and I stepped closer. She held a hand out. "*Don't*. Don't come any closer to me. Not one step. We'll do our show on Saturday, but…it's over. We're over. I can't believe you did this to us."

I froze and held my hands up. "I know this looks bad, but I didn't know she'd be there tonight, and I didn't know you'd be there."

She laughed. "Clearly."

Ignoring her sarcasm, I continued, "I was just about to go back to my room and text you to tell you I couldn't wait till you came to Nashville on Saturday. I wasn't going to bring her back with me, or anyone else, either. I want you. Just you. I didn't sleep with her."

She forced a laugh. It sounded as if it hurt to let out. "Now you say that? It's a little late for denial, Austin."

"It's true!" I grabbed her shoulders. "I didn't do it, Mac."

"I don't believe you," she cried, covering her ears.

"You have to. You have to believe me. You know me." I pulled her hands off her ears. "You know I wouldn't do that to you, don't you?"

She jerked free, stumbling backward. I almost helped steady her, but she shot me a dirty look. I held my hands up in the air to show her I wouldn't touch her. "Oh, of course. It's all a big lie, conjured by the media, even though I *saw* you kissing her and *heard* you asking her to forget anything ever happened between the two of you? To pretend it never happened? But, hey, I'm just supposed to *believe* you?"

"Yes, damn it. You should."

She threw her hands up. "And let me guess, you never told her you wanted more than I'd given you, huh? That's all

LOSING *Us*

a mistake too?"

"I..." I dropped my hands at my sides, rolling them into fists. Her eyes were locked on me, silently begging me to agree with her sarcastic statement. To deny that I'd told another woman I was lonely and confused, but there was no way I was going to lie about that. I refused to mislead her. "I said it, but I was drunk and alone, and an idiot for saying I wanted more. That I wished for more. I didn't. I don't."

She wrapped her arms around herself, hugging tightly. She did that when she was upset, and I'd done that. Upset her even more. "When I'm lonely and miss you, I call you. Or look at photos of us, or...watch videos of us performing together." She closed her eyes, two tears slipping out. "I don't tell other men how lonely I am, and how I want more out of my relationship than what I'm getting with you, and *kiss* them. She's a fan, not your friend. There has to be boundaries in place. Strict boundaries. Treating her as if she means nothing to you is... That's... It's not okay. How would you feel if I did that with another guy?"

I pictured her telling some faceless, nameless guy the things I'd told Diane, some fan who would give his left nut to be able to touch her, and I wanted to flip my shit. She was right, and I knew it, and I didn't have a leg to stand on. If I lost her, the woman I loved...

There would be nothing left in my world except my sister.

I'd be alone, and I'd go back to being the sarcastic, sardonic asshole I'd been before Mac had saved me. The guy I'd been the other night when I'd been a fool and gotten drunk in public. And now I was paying for it. *Man*, was I paying for it. My heart seemed as if it had gone away, and all that remained was a hollow ache in my chest. The last time I'd felt this had been when Mac and I had broken off our arrangement, before we'd become a real couple.

I'd thought I'd never feel it again.

Never feel so alone.

Swallowing past my swollen throat, I glanced past her

shoulder, staring at the driver behind her. Her bodyguard was in there. He glowered at me with death in his eyes. I stared back. It hurt less than looking at her. Seeing what I'd done with a few careless words. "I'm sorry. I've never been with someone as famous as…" I cut myself off, knowing she wouldn't like me saying the end. It had always been her worry, that her fame would be too much for me. It wasn't.

"As me," she said hollowly. "Just say it."

"Okay, yeah," I said, my voice low. "As you. But that doesn't matter to me. And that's not the only thing. *I've* never been famous either. Hell, I don't know what the fuck I'm doing anymore, Mac. I'm sorry I fucked up and said I wished for more than I had. And I'm sorry she was in my room, waiting for me. Sorry you had to see that."

"You told her stuff about us. Private stuff." She closed her eyes and took a shaky breath. "How could you do that?"

I flinched. "I'm sorry. I don't know what I was thinking. I was just wishing that you and I could have more. Together. You know?"

"It's too late. It's…" She licked her lips. "Papa always said to be careful what you wish for, because you just might get it. Well, you got what you wished for. We're done. I hope you find what you're looking for, and that you…you…"

She didn't finish that sentence, and I wouldn't have heard it even if she had. It sounded as if a wind tunnel had opened up in my brain, washing out all sounds but her telling me we were done. Her leaving me. She couldn't leave me.

Didn't she know I needed her?

"Please. Don't." I closed the distance between us. The second I touched her, we both flinched. There had always been a connection between us, and it was undeniably still there. Still as strong as ever, and for some reason that made this whole thing hurt even more. "I love you. I love you so damn much."

She placed her hands on my chest, her bright green eyes shining with tears and pain and regret, and she shook her head. Not as much as I had, I was sure. "Why? Why didn't you

LOSING *Us*

just *call* me? Or FaceTime me?"

"I don't know," I whispered. "Because I'm a fucking idiot. But it doesn't mean I don't love you. I do."

She shook her head slightly. Cameras started clicking, and I knew what that meant. We'd been spotted. "You—" As soon as the first light flashed, she stiffened and cut herself off.

"Trouble in paradise?" one pap asked.

"Give us a kiss!" another shouted. "Show everyone you're okay!"

She stepped out of my arms, head down and hidden from the cameras, and I let her. It might have been the hardest thing I'd ever done, but this wasn't the place to have this conversation. Not with at least ten paps screaming questions at us and blinding us with sporadic flashes.

"The storm's about to hit. Come to my hotel with me," I whispered, keeping my head and voice lowered, just like her. "Or I'll come to your place. We need to talk about this privately. *Please*."

"There's nothing to talk about. You weren't happy with me, obviously, if you're hooking up with random girls and telling our secrets." She shook her head. "I saw the look on your face when she kissed you. You weren't exactly repulsed by her."

"*No*." I'd been in shock. Not in lust. I followed her to her car, shielding her from the cameras. All the fuckers would get was pictures of my back if I had anything to say about it. "I won't let this be over. I love you, and you love me. We can make this work."

She opened her door, and slid in—slamming the door shut behind her. As I reached for the handle, she locked it with a trembling hand. I jerked on the handle anyway, but it was useless. She'd locked me out. Heart wrenching and twisting, I leaned down and locked eyes with her. She didn't look sad anymore. Okay, that wasn't true. She still looked sad, but now she looked resigned too. And that scared the hell out of me.

I stared through the barrier at her, and she watched me with her wide, tear-filled green eyes. Holding my breath, I tapped the window two times, our secret code for I love you, and waited for her to do it back. She didn't move.

She didn't love me anymore, because I'd ruined everything…just like I ruined everything else. I lifted my hand, not trusting myself to drive, and a cab pulled up to the curb almost instantly. I launched myself inside, amidst a shitload of flashing lights. "Follow that black car, *now*."

The cabbie slammed on the gas, and we followed Mac out of Nashville. Within a few minutes, the winds kicked up, and I knew we were about to get lost in the storm. I texted Rachel. She was seventeen now and away from home with her friend's family, but that didn't stop me from worrying about her. I should be with her, not here, stuck in a storm, watching my life slip out of my fingers.

She replied that she was okay, and I tucked the phone into my pocket.

Hard rain hit the roof of the cab, and for a second, I wondered if Mac even knew where she was going. But then the black car pulled up to a dark house in the middle of nowhere, and she climbed out, holding her bag to her chest with a wet face. As soon as the car pulled away, I paid the cab driver and got out.

I remained hidden until the car left so she wouldn't be able to send me away easily. It was time for me to fix what I'd ruined. Time for me to get Mac to understand I'd been an idiot, yes, but that didn't mean I didn't love her. I'd never, ever have acted upon any doubts I'd had about us. And I'd never have cheated on her.

She didn't believe me, but it was true.

The second I'd woken up the morning after I'd foolishly spilled my heart out to Diane, I'd known I made a huge mistake. Mac had always been big about keeping our mouths shut, and our personal life personal, and I was on board with that. But that night? I'd broken all those rules.

But the thing was I'd never known love before. And I'd never been in the public eye like this before either. And being

LOSING *Us*

in love with a country superstar wasn't exactly easy. I was learning how to handle the loneliness and fears, but it was a learning curve.

One I'd fucked up.

But one thing hadn't changed. I loved her, and I needed her in my life. There was no way in hell I was going to let one stupid night of running my mouth ruin what we had. She was sunshine and roses, and I was black thorns and cloudy skies. Without her…

I'd drown in a world of darkness.

CHAPTER *Three*

Mackenzie

The dark winds whipped around furiously, matching my mood. I'd come to Nashville early, hoping to have a romantic reunion with the man I loved, and instead I'd gotten my heart broken. Had he really been so unhappy with me, with our love, that he'd had to tell a strange woman about us? About how he wanted *more*? Had he really needed to *kiss* her? He said he hadn't slept with her, but the trust had been broken. And I didn't believe him anymore. Why would I? I'd caught him red-handed.

This wasn't the first time I'd been cheated on, and I hoped to God it was the last. Every time I let my defenses down and let someone in, let myself fall for a guy, something like this happened. And when it did, the media ate it up like birthday cake. And it always fell down to *me*. What *I'd* done to cause this.

LOSING *Us*

And now it was going to happen again.

Even worse, it had already started. The media knew all about our rocky relationship, and once news of this insanity hit, they'd pick apart the scraps of what was left like vultures. This was going to be the worst breakup ever, and it hurt so much. So freaking much. I loved Austin, and I'd thought he loved me. I'd been so sure…

And look what that certainty had gotten me.

Despite my hope that my crazy lifestyle wouldn't affect our relationship, when I'd been away working, Austin had been wallowing in loneliness and feeling like I wasn't giving him enough of me. I loved him with all my heart and soul.

What more did he want from me?

When my best friends hadn't answered my calls, I'd emailed my publicist and told her about the split. The sooner we planned the best way to announce this, the better. But, God, I didn't want to. I wanted Austin. And the house on twenty-five acres in the middle of nowhere that we'd talked about. And our two kids—a boy and a girl. And our freaking dog and cat.

But now, I'd get none of that. That life would never be lived, because he'd *cheated* on me. Soon, the whole world would know all about my pain. They'd rip it apart, analyze it, come up with reasons for the split, and then tweet the horrible things to me to read. It was over—he was done and I was done—and *oh my God, it hurt so much*.

Hands shaking, I pulled the key out of my bag. I loved this house because it was in the middle of nowhere. Kind of like our dream home, but with not quite enough land. No nearby stores. No cars. No phone. It was like stepping back in time whenever I came home. It let me unplug from the world. Detox. After the news hit, it was bound to be everywhere. That didn't mean I had to see it.

Unlocking the door, I stepped inside and set my bag down just as the skies opened up. The storm had hit, bringing a tornado warning with it. Home sweet home. Maybe a tornado would come and rip me away into Oz. I could use the vacation.

A sound came from behind me, and I spun around, half expecting a wolf or something to be there, ready to pounce. Or maybe a zombie. What I found was even more terrifying. "Austin?" I squeaked, my heart racing even more than it had been. "No. No, no, *no*. You have to go. You're not coming in with me."

I tried to shut the door in his face, but he was too quick. He stepped inside, towering over me. His familiar smell hit me, and I closed my eyes because it hurt. It brought back memories of love-filled evenings, laughter, and sunshine. And now that was all gone.

"I can't," he said, his tone hesitant. "My car left."

I shook my head, knowing there was nothing I could do. The storm had hit, and no driver in his or her right mind would come out here to get him now. Heck, I was already worried about my driver, whom I'd sent back to the city. I couldn't ask another to come. Austin kicked the door shut behind him and took his hat off, shaking his head like a dog. The lights were out, but that didn't stop me from seeing his face. Or those blue eyes of his I loved so freaking much it hurt to see them.

I didn't want him here. Not with *me*.

"You shouldn't have followed me," I said, my voice cracking. "Now we're stuck here together, because of the storm."

"I know. I planned it that way. We need to talk." He stepped closer to me, and I forced myself to stand my ground. "I know I fucked up. I own that. But I'm not giving up on you, on *us*, on everything that we are and could be, because of one fucking night."

"It hurts, Austin." I pressed a hand to my heart. It didn't help. "It hurts too much. I can't."

"I'm sorry. I'm so fucking sorry. But I had to follow you. I'd follow you to the ends of the earth if I had to. I'm not letting you go. Not losing you." He caught my shoulders in his hands and lowered his forehead to mine. "I love you, Mac. I love you so damn much. Believe me. Please…" He tipped my chin up with a trembling hand. "*Please.*"

LOSING *Us*

My lids drifted shut. I knew I should move away. Kick him. Punch him. Scream at him. But I couldn't move. I was mesmerized by his touch. His soft voice. *Him*. He lowered his mouth to mine, moving slow enough to give me a chance—a thousand chances—to move away or say no. I didn't do either. I couldn't. A broken sound escaped me the second his lips touched mine.

Because I *was*. Broken. *So* badly.

When he stepped closer, closing me in his embrace and looming over me, a hundred images of us together flashed before me in some horrible montage. Us snorkeling. Kissing in the rain. Me telling him I loved him. The way he'd looked on stage for the first time on tour with me. But the last image, of him kissing that blonde in his dressing room, ripped me out of the kiss. And out of his arms.

I stumbled back, covering my mouth. "Don't. Just...don't."

A flash of lightning struck just in time for me to see the pain flash across his eyes. "Mac—"

Shaking my head, I pressed two fingers to my lips. I wanted to fall into his arms and blindly believe that everything would be okay, that we'd be able to fix us, but I couldn't. I'd ignored logic and all rational thought once before, when I'd believed we would be happy together, and that he'd never hurt me. I couldn't do it again. Not twice. "You told her you weren't happy. Broke my trust by letting a stranger into a relationship. A stranger who couldn't wait to sell that information to the media."

He blinked. "What? What do you mean?"

"She—" I cut myself off. It didn't matter what she'd done. Not really. It mattered what he'd done. He'd betrayed me in ways I could never forgive. Not just by kissing another girl, or maybe sleeping with her, but by telling her how unhappy he was with me. By telling her I wasn't *enough*. I already knew that, but to hear him say it? Yeah, that hurt more than the kiss itself. "Just...just leave me alone. It's done."

I escaped up the stairs, heading for my bedroom. I bolted

into what was once my sanctuary, slamming the door shut behind me. The second I clicked the lock into place, I slid down the door, crouching on the floor in front of the only thing saving me from falling right back into Austin's arms without another thought.

He'd said he was new to this whole love thing, but so was I. I'd never been in love before him, and I didn't know what to do now that it had all fallen apart. He'd been the one who had convinced me he'd be fine with my tours, recordings, and red carpet appearances. I'd trusted him, despite the small voice in the back of my head screaming that I was a fool. I'd ignored it and listened to him.

And now he'd said I was too busy for him.

That I wasn't enough.

Dropping my forehead on my knees, I hugged my legs tightly to my chest to ease the pain inside. And I let myself fully cry. Didn't he know how much I loved him? Needed him? How could he do this to me? To us? How could he have kissed that girl? Touched her? He'd said he hadn't, but what if he'd slept with her? What if he'd lied about that, too, just like he'd lied about being happy with me? And what the heck were we supposed to do now that we were stuck in this house together, but not *together*? How were we going to survive this storm? *Or* the one raging outside?

Footsteps came up outside the door, and I covered my mouth, muffling the sobs. He didn't need to know how badly he'd hurt me, or how weak I was right now. Something hit the door. His forehead, maybe.

"I'm sorry, Mac. So fucking sorry. But I didn't sleep with her. I swear it. And I'm not going anywhere. We're going to fix this. I refuse to lose you. To lose...us."

I didn't answer. I couldn't. Instead, I pressed my hand more firmly to my mouth, holding back the tears trying to escape. It was a losing battle, and I knew it.

"I know I fucked up, but I love you, and I know you love me. We can..." He paused. "We can make it through this,

LOSING Us

damn it. I'm sorry I got drunk like that, and I'm even sorrier that I ruined your trust. But I'm going to win it back, because when you love someone, you don't just walk away. You don't give up. I might not know much about love, but at least I know that. You know that, right, Mac?"

I bit down on the back of my hand so I didn't say anything I'd regret. Anything I might want to take back. And, as hard as it was, I didn't answer his plea.

He sighed. "I'm not giving up on us. I'll let you be alone now, since you want that, but I'm not going away. And I'm not going to stop apologizing, for the rest of my life if I have to, for hurting you like this. I'm sorry."

He waited, maybe hoping I'd open the door for him, but then sighed again. His footsteps retreated, and I sagged against the door, clutching my stomach and staring at the empty bed. I didn't know what to think. What to say. What to believe.

So I said, and did, nothing.

He kept saying he hadn't cheated on me, hadn't slept with her, but that conversation had seemed awfully damning to me, despite his assurances. People didn't pretend "nothing" happened if nothing happened. End of story. And they didn't kiss like that. Images of him, with his hands all over random girls with that silly grin on his face, hit me hard. Had I been fooling myself into thinking they were normal pictures? If he got drunk with one of his fans, who was to say he hadn't done it again and again and again? Who was to say that Diane was the only girl who'd felt she was welcome to wait in his dressing room topless? Who was to say that had been the first time?

Not me.

Chin up, sweetheart. Life isn't so bad.

Lifting my head, I dragged my hands across my cheeks and rose to my feet unsteadily. My father's voice still echoed in my head. He was right, and always had been. Enough crying and pouting. It was time to stiffen that upper lip and get back to being me. Yes, it ached that he'd hurt me, but I wasn't a little girl anymore. And like Fergie once said… Big girls don't cry.

I flicked on the bedroom light switch at the same time a bolt of lightning shook the house. With a *pop* and a whir, the lights went out. Closing my eyes, I muttered, "You've got to be kidding me."

Why hadn't I brought my purse upstairs? If I had it, I could use the flashlight on my phone to see. But alas, I hadn't. I'd been too busy running away from Austin.

Shaking my head, I felt my way across the room, trying to reach my bed. I had a flashlight in my nightstand drawer, so if I could get there, I'd be able to see again. A flash of lightning hit again, and it illuminated the room for a split second. I bolted across the room, taking advantage of it while I could. But as nature provides the light, it also takes it away all too quickly. I banged my toe on the chair next to my dresser.

Howling, I hopped on one foot and clutched my shoeless foot in my hand. I'd kicked off my heels mid-cry earlier. "Ow!"

"Shit! Are you okay?" Austin shouted out from somewhere downstairs. "*Mac!*"

Pettily, I didn't want to answer him. But I knew he'd come up if I didn't, so I swallowed my pride and called out, "I-I'm fine."

"Stay where you are." His voice sounded closer now. "I'll come get you."

Pressing my lips together, I fought the urge to tell him to go kiss his own ass. "No. Stay down there."

"What? I—" A crash, followed by a muffled cry…and a thump.

"Austin?" I called out, my heart pounding loudly in my ears. "Are you okay?"

He didn't answer, making my heart accelerate even more. He might have cheated on me, and he'd broken my heart and my trust, but that didn't change the fact that I loved him with all of mine. And he might be hurt down there.

"Austin?" Nothing. "Crap."

Fumbling across the room, I managed to find my nightstand without any more bodily injury. When I pushed

LOSING *Us*

the button on the bottom of the flashlight, nothing happened. Dead batteries.

"Son of a bitch whoreson," I snarled, stealing one of Austin's most commonly used phrases when he was pissed off. I wasn't much for swearing myself, so I didn't have my own to pull out of my head. Tossing the useless thing on my bed, I held my arms out in front of me and moved through the darkness as quickly as I could.

"I'm coming!" I called out, even though he wasn't answering me. *Why* wasn't he answering me? "Austin!"

I finally reached the door, and opened it. The hallway was even darker than my room, since there were no windows. Stretching my arms to either side, I felt my way down the hallway, swallowing hard. If Austin was being quiet, he might be hurt. Like, actually hurt. "Austin?" I whispered.

Nothing.

When I reached the top of the stairs, I gripped the railing and went down, one careful step at a time. My palms began to sweat, because I knew if he wasn't answering me, if he was letting me worry like this, then it could mean something bad. Really bad. I reached the bottom of the stairs…

And I tripped.

Hitting the hardwood floor hard with both hands, I groaned and rolled over, feeling around for what I'd caught my foot on. When I touched warm flesh, I cried out.

I'd tripped over Austin.

My hand came back wet, and I held it up to my face. Had the roof leaked, or rain somehow gotten in? Or was it…?

The lightning flashed, and I stared at my hand in horror.

It was *red*.

My heart wrenched painfully. Austin was unconscious and bleeding, and I couldn't even see him to discern how bad it was. I had to do something to help him.

Or he might…

"No. No, no, no, *no*."

CHAPTER
Four

Austin

As I opened my eyes, the light hurt like hell. Slamming them shut instantly, I groaned. The second thing I realized was that groaning hurt too. And the third, I was lying at the bottom of the stairs. Why was I…?

With almost as much pain, my memory came crashing back to me.

Mac had cried out, and I'd been trying to get to her. But it had been dark, and I'd tripped over a damn cord, slamming my head on one of the wooden stairs. Turned out my head wasn't as hard as I liked to think, or as everyone told me.

I'd lost consciousness.

The wind whipped outside furiously, and it sounded as if something flew against the front door. What the hell was going on out there? A fucking tornado?

"Mac," I whispered, lifting a hand and pressing it to my

throbbing head. It didn't matter. I had to get to her. Had to make sure she was okay. "I'm coming."

Forcing my eyes open, I blinked against the light again. Wait…light? Where was it coming from? I forced myself to focus. Candles. Lots of candles. If there were candles lit, then Mac must have come down and found me like this, which meant she was okay. I sagged back against the floor. "Mac?"

I lowered my hand and blinked at it. Blood.

Oh. Fucking great.

My angel came around the corner, a flashlight in her mouth and a first-aid kit in her arms. She looked pale, and her mouth was pinched tight with worry. When she saw me watching her, she jumped a tiny bit, and hurried over. "You're awake," she said softly, falling to my side on her knees.

"Yeah." I touched my forehead again and flinched. "My head hurts like a bitch, though. I fell."

"Yeah, I know. And I'm sure it does. Stop touching it," she said, ripping open the kit. She'd placed the flashlight on the floor, face up. "I'm going to bandage it up, but we'll have to watch you for any signs of a concussion."

"I've had tons of those," I muttered, closing my eyes. "I don't have one."

"You don't know that."

"Yeah, I pretty much do. Even if I have one, like I said, I've had tons, so I wouldn't worry too much. I survived them all. I'd probably survive this one."

She looked at me out of the corner of her eye. "Tons?"

"Yeah." I hesitated. This wasn't a subject I generally opened up about, but this was my Mac. She deserved an explanation. "My dad liked hitting my face. Said I was too pretty for my own good, and I needed a few scars to 'man me up.'"

A small sound escaped her, and she rested a hand on my chest. "Austin…"

"Yeah?"

"Look at me," she said, her voice soft and tender.

I squared my jaw and opened my eyes, meeting hers

without shame or embarrassment. I'd once been too prideful to admit such things, but she'd changed me for the better. She'd saved me, and now I accepted that it wasn't my fault my father had been a dick.

But now I might be losing her.

I could take a million beatings from my asshole dad, but I'd never survive life without her at my side. So I refused to lose her. "I *am* looking at you. Believe me, I am."

She pressed a finger to an old scar under my chin. "This one?" She touched the light scar under my left eye. "And this one? Both from him?"

I nodded once. "All of them."

"God." She swallowed hard and averted her eyes. "Your dad was an asshole."

"No argument here. That's where I get it from."

"Don't say that," she snapped, her movements jerky. "Don't ever say that. You're *nothing* like him."

"But I—" I tried to cock my brow, but it hurt like hell. Hissing, I slammed my brow back down. "Shit, that hurt."

"I know. Here." She rummaged behind her and a wrapper crinkled. "Eat this."

I glanced down at her hand. It was three crackers. "Why?"

"I'm going to give you pain pills, but I don't want it to hurt your stomach."

Not taking the crackers, I shook my head. I didn't want my brain to be foggy. I needed to be on point tonight. "I'm fine. I don't need—"

"*Austin.*" She shoved them beneath my nose. "Eat. Them. Now."

I took them, kind of liking this bossy side of her. It was hot. "Yes, ma'am."

As I munched on the crackers while surreptitiously watching her, she pulled out hydrogen peroxide. I'd never used the shit before. When Dad had hit me, I'd just cleaned myself up the best I could, then crawled under my blanket and hid from the world, in case he came back for seconds. I'd bring

Rachel with me and we'd hide and pretend we were other people.

Anyone but us. Anything but reality.

I wanted to do that again, but with Mac in my arms.

Mac faced me, her face even paler than before. The soft candlelight highlighted her soft curves and cheekbones. The red lips I loved so damn much were pursed in concentration. She smoothed her hair off her face. It was brown again.

How had I not noticed that earlier?

"Your hair is brown again."

She glanced at me before turning her attention back to the peroxide. "Yeah. It's been a year, so I thought it would be fun."

When I'd met her, her hair had been brown. She'd been trying to fit in with the crowds and be normal. I'd known who she was right away, but I hadn't told her.

It had almost made me lose her before I even had her.

"I like it. You look pretty. You always do."

Her grip tightened on the bottle. "Thanks. I'm sorry, but this is going to hurt."

"It can't be that bad."

She opened the cap. "Surely you used this a lot, too, as a kid?"

"Nope. Never." I ate my last cracker and swallowed. "All done eating. Do I get a cookie now, for good behavior?"

"No. You get pills." Taking a deep breath, she handed me two capsules. "Take these."

I did. After she handed me a bottle of water, I swallowed them and lifted my head, trying to see what she had behind her. She had a little makeshift hospital there. "You're not planning on stitching me up on your own, are you?"

"No. God, no." She looked a little green at the mere suggestion. "The wound isn't deep, so I think it'll heal on its own. It's mostly superficial, but head wounds bleed a lot. At least, I think they do. It'll scar, though."

I shrugged as best as I could. She was acting so steady and calm. I wasn't sure what that meant, but I didn't like it. I was a fucking mess, and she was tending my wounds as if she'd gone to med school instead of the fucking Grammys. "My dad would be happy. He's probably laughing, wherever he is right now."

In hell, more than likely.

"I'm sure he would," she muttered.

Turning my head to the side, I saw my hat in a puddle of blood. It wasn't just a hat to me. It was a symbol of all I'd accomplished when I'd taken over as Rachel's guardian. It was us. Our life together. And now it was covered in blood…again.

"Shit." I reached for it but couldn't touch it. "My hat. I need my hat."

"Leave it there. I'll wash it once the power comes back," she said quickly, still opening things and ripping open packages of gauze. "It'll be fine, and if not, you can buy another one."

"I can't. It'll stain."

She scooted closer, peroxide and cotton swab in hand. "It's just a hat."

"No, it's not *just a hat*." I swallowed hard, my eyes locked on the stuff in her hand. It looked dangerous. It was in a dark bottle that had all sorts of weird labels on it. "Rachel bought it for me when she was fourteen, after…"

Right after our father had tried to kill her.

Mac's hand trembled a little bit. She knew exactly what that meant, even if I hadn't finished the sentence. I didn't need to. "Oh. I see. Well, after we're finished here, I'll wash it."

"Thank you," I said, my voice a lot softer than I'd intended. After clearing my throat, I asked, "What are you going to do with that stuff, anyway?"

"Clean the wound," she said, tipping the bottle upside down on the swab. "Technically, we should pour it over the wound and keep doing so until it stops bubbling, but I don't want to make you move yet, and I don't want to get it in your eyes and hair. Again, sorry, but this is going to hurt."

It bubbled? Well, shit, if it bubbled, it couldn't be bad. Bubbles were never scary. Hell, kids loved them. "It's fine. Do

LOSING *Us*

it."

"Sorry," she whispered again. The second she touched the cotton ball to my head, it felt as if she'd poured scalding liquid into the wound. "So sorry."

"Jesus fucking Christ," I growled, slamming my eyes shut. "Mother fucker son of a bitch whore son *fuck*."

A small sound escaped her, and I couldn't tell if it was a laugh or a groan. Maybe both. "I used some of your curses earlier when I stubbed my toe."

I gritted my teeth. Slow breaths in, slow breaths out. "Did it help?"

"No." She paused. "Did it help you?"

"*No*." She took her hand away, and I sagged against the stairs. "Damn, if my dad knew how much that shit hurt, he would have made me use it instead of telling me to wash the blood off of myself with soap and water."

Her leg stiffened next to my arm. "What a—"

"Asshole. I know." I opened my eyes. "Are we done here?"

"No. We need to do it again."

"Shiiiiit."

"Sorry," she whispered again. "So sorry."

It didn't stop her from doing it, though. She pressed another wet ball against the wound, but this time I was prepared for the pain. I didn't make a sound. "It's fine. I deserve it," I said through my clenched teeth. "For hurting you. This is only one of my punishments to come, I'm sure."

She swiped the cotton ball across my forehead. I expected her to shut me out. Tell me to stop talking, but she didn't. "Tell me the truth. Please…I need the truth, no matter how hard it might be to say. Did you…did you…cheat on me with that girl?"

I caught her wrist. It was so small in my hand. "No. I swear it on everything I've ever held dear in my life, I did *not* cheat on you. I couldn't have."

"You couldn't have?" she asked, biting down on her tongue like she always did when she was thinking way too hard. "Or you didn't? Do you even remember that night? Everything you did and said?"

Damn it, she had to ask that, didn't she? It seeded that small kernel of doubt that I'd been trying to ignore. The one that pointed out that I *had* been drunk off my ass.

"I don't remember *everything*," I admitted, knowing I was screwing myself over with my complete honesty, but she didn't deserve half-truths. "But I know me, and I wouldn't have done that to you. Not in a million years."

"But you…you remember talking with that girl. Intimately."

"Yes." I let go of her and dropped my arm back to my side. "I'd been drinking. Though at the time, it hadn't seemed like I had that much. And I had a headache. And I hadn't talked to you in a while, so I was feeling sentimental. And I opened up to the wrong person, yes, but I didn't sleep with her. I couldn't have."

"You keep saying that," she said, tossing the cotton ball back down. "But you can't remember everything, and you were unhappy and drunk. So really, anything could have happened. Because I was gone, and you were missing me *so much*. And you wanted more."

"Yes. Exactly." I nodded, but it hurt too much, so I stopped. "It wasn't that I was saying I wanted more from *her*. I wanted more of you. That's it. It's just because I love you so much, and I was frustrated because I never see you, but I'll be fine. It was a weak night. That's all."

For some reason, that didn't seem to make her feel better. "How long have you known this girl?" She pulled out another cotton ball and soaked it in peroxide. Jesus. "A week? A month? A year?"

I scanned my brain for an answer, but it wasn't being very helpful right now. All I could think, and feel, was my pain. And it wasn't only from my head. I gritted my teeth. "She comes to all of my shows, and has since I toured with you. She's always there. I guess she's a groupie of sorts…"

She set the cotton ball on the wound, swiping it gently, her

LOSING *Us*

jaw tight. "So a few months."

"Yes." I forced myself to relax and ignore the pain. "She's always there…"

"And I'm not," she said hollowly.

"That's not what I meant. I'm okay with you being busy, and you know it." I caught her hand again. She didn't pull away. "I knew what I was getting into when we fell in love. You're a busy woman, and that's awesome."

She tossed the third ball aside. When she capped the peroxide, I let out a sigh of relief. That form of torture was over, at least. "The thing is, it's easy to say you are okay with it, and a different thing to actually *be* okay with it."

"But I am. Okay. With it."

She pulled out a bandage that looked like a butterfly Band-Aid. I'd used those a lot as a kid. "Yeah. Sure."

"Mac—"

"No. Enough talking about this," she said, her voice not even wobbling the littlest bit. "The truth is, you're not okay with it, and you want more. You even told a *groupie* as much."

I reached for her, but she moved away. "But—"

"Want to know the worst part about all of this? You don't even realize why I don't like talking to the media. Why I asked you to keep our personal life personal."

"It was one time," I said, frustration making my voice hard. "Haven't you ever messed up once before? I mean, shit, Mac. I'm trying here."

She let out a small laugh. "You know, I read almost those same exact words in a magazine article on the plane, but I thought it was normal tabloid junk." She gently placed the bandage on my head, then clapped her hands together twice, as if she dusted them off. I got the distinct impression she was dusting me off her hands…and out of her life. She stood. "Apparently, your new friend likes to talk to the media even more than she likes to strip naked in your dressing room."

I struggled to sit, but I couldn't get my balance. "She's not my friend. I don't even like her, or know her. It was all a mistake. A stupid, drunken mistake."

"That's too bad," she said, holding a hand out to help me. "It's really just too freaking bad."

"You're angry again," I said flatly.

"I never stopped being angry," she replied, wiggling her fingers. "You want help or not?"

I slid my hand into hers. The electrical spark that existed between us hit me, and I tightened my grip on hers. She pulled away slightly. "I'm sorry, Mac."

"I know." She locked eyes with me. "I am too."

I struggled to my feet, but the room spun. I swayed a bit, trying to catch my bearings. "Shit."

"Come on." She wrapped her arm around my waist and pressed her curves against me. "Let's get you on the couch before you crack your head open again. Your head might be hard, but it's not *that* hard."

I let her lead me into the living room. As we walked, she pressed even closer to me, her soft curves tantalizing me. Despite my aching head, my body responded to her with ferocious enthusiasm. It had been too long since she'd touched me, and man, I'd missed her. Missed the way that she fit against my body, all softness where I was hard.

When we reached the couch, I let go of her reluctantly and yawned, my lids feeling suspiciously heavy. "I'm just going to crash. It's been a long day."

A day when I'd flown into Nashville, performed, and then almost, maybe, broken up with the only girl I'd ever loved… besides Rachel. And would only ever love.

But we weren't broken up yet. I'd fix it after some shut-eye.

"You can't go to sleep." She placed a blanket over me. "You have a possible concussion, remember? Stay awake, Austin."

"Yes, Mother," I muttered, my eyes opening the tiniest fraction. "I'm up."

"Good. Stay that way. I'm going to go clean up all the blood and stuff." I watched her go. She picked up my hat as she went, staring down at it. "And I'll soak this in detergent so the blood

LOSING Us

doesn't set in. Do *not* fall asleep."

"You worry too much."

"You don't worry enough," she countered, shooting me a warning glare.

And then she was gone.

"I slept through worse before." I closed my eyes. "I'll do so again."

The couch pillow and blanket smelled like her. I inhaled her scent like a starved man and turned off my mind. Tried to forget all the horrible things that had happened tonight. I was done with this day. Tomorrow, I'd fight for us. Tomorrow, I'd figure out how to get her to forgive me, and everything would be okay.

But tonight? I needed some fucking sleep.

CHAPTER *Five*

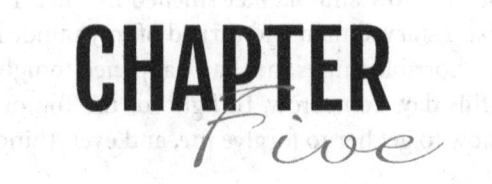

Mackenzie

I ran the water, filling up the sink with soapy cold suds. The power was out, so there was no hot water to be had. Heck, I didn't know which was better for bloodstains, anyway. I hadn't exactly been much of a bleeder as a kid. The worst I'd suffered was a nasty bike spill on the sidewalk that had gashed open my knee, and my dad had cleaned it up for me before buying me ice cream at the shop.

Hearing Austin talk about his own twisted childhood so matter-of-factly had hit me hard. He'd had such a horrible upbringing. I'd thought mine had been bad, with my drug addict mother stealing money from me and all, but before that, she'd been okay. Not mother-of-the-year material, but not like Austin's father. I'd known his childhood was rough, but he didn't often share glimpses of it like that.

Just here and there, and when he spoke of it, he acted as if it was completely normal. As if every kid got beat up because he looked too "pretty." It broke my heart. He'd known so little love in his life, and I knew he loved me. I knew he would never intentionally hurt me, so I kept trying to remind myself of that. But despite *knowing*...

It still hurt.

What really stung, though, was that my worst fears were coming true. Back when I'd met Austin, and fallen for him, I'd told him we would never work because he lived in Florida, and I was always on the go. He'd assured me he didn't care, that he was willing to deal with my crazy life, and I'd thrown caution to the wind—and myself—in his arms.

For a while there, I'd thought he'd been right. That we would be okay, even though we barely saw one another. That we could make it past all the fears and doubts and be happy. Really, really happy. I'd thought we could have it all. The whole relationship had played out in front of my eyes. A happy dating life, followed by a romantic proposal. A lavish wedding with a pure white wedding dress, and then the life that came after. The one with the house and kids and pets. The life I'd thought we both wanted. But then he'd dropped the bomb on me that he wanted *more*. That I wasn't giving him enough of me.

The thing was, between school and my career, I worked almost fifteen hours a day. Two hours went to eating three well-balanced meals a day, and another hour went to the gym. That didn't leave a whole lot of time for being a dedicated girlfriend and, you know, sleeping. I didn't *have* more of myself to give.

As it was, I was already stretched thinner than any normal human should be, and I was barely holding on to my sanity. If he wanted more, then he had every right to do so.

But he wouldn't be able to get more from me.

So that meant I'd been right to break up with him, whether or not he'd actually cheated on me. When he'd fallen in love with me, he probably hadn't fully realized the type of life I led, and I didn't blame him for second-guessing what we had. I agreed. It wasn't enough. I'd hoped he could be a permanent part of my international tours, and we could see the world together, but it wasn't possible because of his commitments to Rachel. Commitments I admired more than anything else. Which meant we weren't possible. As much as I loved him...

I had to let him go.

And I would do it, if that was what was best for him. Letting him go wasn't best for me, but he deserved a chance at a real girlfriend. One who lived in Florida. One who could love him as much as he deserved to be loved. I loved him more than I'd ever thought possible, but I wasn't *there* most of the time.

And I certainly understood, no matter how much it hurt, that I wasn't enough anymore. Sometimes, like the song said, love just wasn't enough.

It wasn't enough now, obviously.

Shutting off the water, I swished his hat around in it and dried off my hands. Tossing the rag onto the counter, I followed the candles into the living room. On any other night, this would be a romantic setting, but tonight it was all falling apart.

I was losing him. Losing us.

Lightning flashed again, and a boom of thunder shook the house. Things were still raging out there, and God only knew how long it would be before it calmed down. Stopping outside the living room, I took a second to compose myself. He didn't need to see how much it hurt to know it was over. "I think your hat will be okay. I—"

Was wasting my time talking.

He'd fallen asleep after I'd told him not to. Damn him. If he had a concussion, he didn't need sleep. He needed to stay awake. Snatching the flashlight off the floor, I stalked across the room and stopped at his side. As I crouched beside him, I froze just short of shaking him. He looked so...so... Peaceful.

His breaths were even, and he looked younger in his sleep. Softer. I hadn't seen him sleep in so long. His lips were pursed and his brow furrowed, as if he'd been having a nightmare. I reached out and gently brushed my fingers over his forehead. He instantly settled in, the creases fading away. His dark brown brows were hard and slanted, but I knew underneath those lids were the bluest eyes I'd ever seen.

Trailing my fingers down his cheek, I traced the curve of his chin dimple. It had been one of the first things I'd noticed about him, followed by his blue eyes and dark tattoos. Then I'd talked to him, and I'd fallen under his spell. I'd thought I would never have to climb back out again. I guess I'd been wrong.

I closed my eyes. The headline of the article I'd read on the plane flashed before my eyes. The one Diane had sold to *Star*. *"Rock Star Austin Murphy wants out! See why he'll break it off with America's Sweetheart."*

It had gone on to say he wanted to be wild and free, and explore his newfound stardom, rock-star style. Drinks, girls, and rock and roll. If the rest of the article had been true—the part about him wanting more from me—then he'd probably said the rest of those things. He might not remember it or admit it...

But it's how he felt, and he couldn't erase that.

Even if my heart didn't want to accept it yet, my mind had already done what I needed to do. He needed to be set free, because he wouldn't leave me. He was too honorable to do it. I had to do it for him. Tears rolled down my cheeks, and I sniffed. He was asleep, so I'd let myself have this last moment of tears, and then I'd do what my father always told me when I'd been upset as a little girl.

Pick up my toys, and move on. Just like life always did.

I would miss him so much, but it was for the best. For him, anyway. Not me. But I had to believe he'd thank me later. He'd get to cut loose and have fun. Screw all the Dianes in the world, and then more. If that's what he really wanted, then he'd get it. And that was that.

Pushing off the couch, I headed across the room to my purse. Tears blurred my vision, but I ignored them. I pulled my phone out and broke one of my rules in this house—I activated my hotspot. As the Internet powered up, two missed calls from my best friends popped up. They'd been trying to return my earlier calls.

I opened my texts and pulled up the group iMessage between Quinn, Cassie, and myself. There were a few texts asking me if I was okay, and how my reunion with Austin had gone. I swallowed hard and typed. *I broke up with Austin. Remember that article I told you about? The one that said he wanted out of the relationship?*

A few seconds passed, and then Quinn said, *Yeah, but it's just the usual tabloid fodder.*

Cassie replied, *Right. Just crap.*

But it wasn't. The source is credible, and Austin actually said that stuff. He wants more, and I can't give it to him. I...I saw him with another girl. He claimed nothing happened, but she's the one he talked to about this. She's the source.

ASSHOLE! Quinn said in all caps.

Jerk! Cassie threw in.

A small smile came out. My girls always had my back. I'd had Cassie's, too, when all that drama went down a few months ago. *He isn't, though. I don't blame him for wanting more, not really. And he didn't break up with me, I broke up with him. I think I need to. He wants to be free...so I'm going to give it to him.*

Are you sure this is what you want? Cassie asked.

No. I don't want it. But he does...so I'm going to give it to him.

Think about it first, Quinn typed. *Before you jump in, think about it real long. It's a big decision to make for the both of you.*

I already told my publicist. The decision was made the second he decided I wasn't enough. I'm setting him free, and he'll thank me later. I'm sure of it, or I wouldn't be doing it.

Mac... Cassie typed.

I don't know... Quinn typed at the same time.

But I do. It's done.

After a few more exchanges in which I promised to let them

LOSING *Us*

both know how everything was going, I said my goodbyes and opened up my email. There was an email from my PR person, so I opened it up. All it said was: *Are you SURE?*

No, of course not. I didn't want this at all. But he'd been so miserable that he may or may not have cheated on me, and then forgotten about it. And so miserable he'd complained to a groupie about our relationship. My thumb hovered over the screen, and I took a deep breath. I didn't want to do this...

But I should.

I walked over to Austin, my thumb still hovering over my screen. If only there was a sign I was doing the right thing. Something to tell me that I should follow through with my plan, and break it off for his own good. Because I was wavering. Maybe I should keep trying. Keep fighting...

On the table next to him, his phone lit up with a message, and I glanced down out of habit. The message, of course, was from Diane. And it had a heart emoticon next to it. He'd *saved* her number in his phone. My heart wrenched, and I closed my eyes.

I shouldn't read it, but I was going to anyway. This was the sign I'd been asking for, even if it wasn't the one I'd been hoping for. Slowly, I bent down, picked it up, and read the message on the lock screen.

Sorry if I got you in trouble with the old lady. And sorry for spilling the beans about that night we shared. That was personal, and I shouldn't have told anyone, like you asked me to. Let me know when you're back in Florida, so I can make it up to you... personally. ;)

Dropping the phone back to the table, I closed my eyes and a small, shattered sound escaped me. Just when I'd thought I couldn't break any more, life proved me wrong. He'd said nothing had happened between the two of them, but I didn't think that was the case. Not anymore. Fans didn't have your number, and have their name in your phone with a freaking heart emoticon. And they definitely didn't call your girlfriend the "old lady" and apologize for "spilling the beans."

I'd never, ever given a fan my phone number, or made them think they were someone who could call me and text me. There had to boundaries. Rules. Or people could get hurt. If I'd needed one more reason to let him go...

I'd just gotten it. Loud and clear.

Waking my phone, I jotted off a quick reply to my publicist and hit send before I backed down. As my fingers flew over the screen, my tears dried up. It might hurt like hell, but I knew what I had to do. Knew what needed to be done. It was up to me now to get it that way. To accept what was staring me in the face.

It was time to let Austin go.

CHAPTER
Six

Austin

I ran through the dark streets of Miami, chasing Mac as she tried to escape me. My heart pounded hard, and I increased my pace, knowing if she got away I'd never see her again. I'd lose her.

"Come back!" I called out, pumping my arms and legs so fast it hurt. "Don't leave!"

"Austin," I heard from a distance, as if through a wall or something. I'd know that voice anywhere, and I knew who was shaking my shoulder. It was Mackenzie. How was that possible when she was right in front of me, running away? "*Austin!*"

I jerked awake, which hurt my head, and blinked at the ceiling, my breaths coming ragged and uneven. "What? What's wrong?"

"I told you to stay awake." She lifted a flashlight, grabbed hold of my head—which pressed her wrist up against my mouth—and shone the light into it. The brightness hurt my already aching head. "You were having a nightmare, crying out in your sleep."

I closed my eyes, swallowing hard. I still couldn't breathe, as if I'd actually been running. "Yeah, I know."

"What was it about?" she asked, her touch soft.

"Losing you."

She froze, but then went back to doing whatever it was she was doing. "Stay still. I need to check you over."

She was obviously still concerned I had a concussion, but I was 99 percent certain she was wrong. My head hurt, and my heart hurt, but that was it.

My brain, unfortunately, was just fine.

"Do I have a choice?" I mumbled against her wrist. If she hadn't been so angry with me, I'd have licked it or nipped at it. "I told you, I'm fine."

"Your pupils are responding nicely," she said, ignoring me. Her tone was professional, as if she did this for a living. Again, it scared the shit out of me. She was acting as if we were already done. We weren't. She shifted to the other eye, and I turned away from the light because it hurt. "I told you to stay still."

Her face was mere inches from mine, and the need to close the distance between us, to kiss her until she forgot why she was mad at me, was overpowering. I swallowed back the impulse, knowing it wouldn't be welcome. "Do you even know what you're looking for?"

"Yes." Lowering the flashlight, she flicked it off. Again, she sat there beside me, so close I could touch her, but unable to do so. "So far, so good. But you still need to stay awake for a little while longer, just to be safe."

I nodded once, fingering the bandage she'd placed over my wound. "My hat?"

"It's soaking. I think it'll be okay." She smoothed the blanket over me. "How's your head feeling?"

"Better than the rest of me." I caught her gaze. "Thank you

for taking care of me and my hat."

She nodded but didn't speak.

Fear, of the like I'd never known, pierced through my chest. She'd shut me out already. I could see it. Hear it. Feel it. "Can we talk?"

"It's a free country," she said, her tone as even as before. "Talk all you want."

"You have to understand...I didn't mean to hurt you, Mac."

She fidgeted with the blanket. "I know, but you did. I had to hear you were unhappy through a magazine, and through some other girl. You told *her* before you told *me*."

Shit, I got it now. Got why she was so upset.

I should have come to her first. Told her I missed her and wanted to see her, but I hadn't wanted to stress her out more than she already was.

Despite what she thought, I *knew* she was a busy woman. I got it. So I hadn't wanted to add more stress to her life by being a clingy boyfriend. Fuck that shit. She didn't need me weighing her down. I was supposed to help her, not make her life harder.

I sagged against the pillows. They still smelled like her. Damn pillows. "I didn't want you to worry."

She stood up and shifted her weight on her feet. "What really sucks isn't that you didn't tell me, or who you told before me, but that you feel that way at all. Because in the next few months, we'd see each other even less."

I swallowed hard at her use of past tense. As if it was already done, and it had been officially announced and everything. It hadn't, and if I had anything to say about it, it never would. "I know that."

"But you don't. Not really. The real issue is this: We can't fix the thing you're most upset about. If I was being bitchy, or you felt that I should call you more, then I could work on that. But I know my schedule, and you know yours, and it isn't going to get any better. *I can't give you more*."

"I don't need more. I'll be okay," I said quickly, knowing

where she was going with this. And I wasn't going to let her go there. Fuck that. "And that other part isn't true, either. We'll have more time together in a year or so, because Rachel will graduate and go off to college."

"And until then, you live in Florida, and have to stay there most of the year, and I travel all over hell and back. And I spend most of my time here in Nashville."

She flexed her fingers and stepped back from me. It felt as if she did more than move away from me physically. I felt it deep in my heart, as corny as that might sound coming from me. Before I'd met her, I hadn't even been sure if I *had* a heart.

"We'll make it work. It'll be okay."

She shook her head. "It's not. And we won't. Soon, you will be travelling too. You think we'll have more time together, but we won't. Your album will take off, and you'll become even more popular than you already are, and then you'll be doing your own tour, which is *great*. You deserve all of that. But we'll…we'll fall apart even more. If you couldn't handle this now, you wouldn't be able to handle it then."

Shaking my head, I grabbed one of her hands in between mine. "No. I refuse to believe it. We can make it through all the craziness. I'm sure of it."

"I once was too." She bit her lip and pulled free. "But now, I'm not. There's a reason no relationships in Hollywood work. Singers aren't spared that curse. And…and…you hurt me, Austin. A lot. You can't just…I can't…"

"I know," I whispered.

"She texted you. That girl."

I winced. I hadn't even realized I'd given her my number. "How do you know it was her?"

"You saved her in your phone," she said, her voice hollow.

"I did?"

Her gaze flickered over to me, then left again. She stared out the window. "You did. With a heart next to it."

Now I knew she was full of shit. I didn't put hearts next to any goddamn thing. And if I were going to put them next to someone's name, it would have been hers or Rachel's. They were the only ones who had my heart in their hands. "The hell I did."

"I saw it." Her eyes flashed angrily at me, but the rest of her face remained calm. "So...yeah. She wants you to let her know when you're back in Florida, and she's sorry she got you in trouble. She should have kept your night together a secret, like you asked her to."

I sat up and tossed the blanket aside. "I didn't sleep with that woman. I swear it. You believe me, right?"

But the thing was, I didn't remember anything from that night. That's how drunk I'd been. The last thing I remembered was drinking a little too much and spilling my guts. I'd thought I'd gone to my room to sleep it all off, but what if I hadn't?

What if I'd done the unthinkable?

My gut churned at the mere thought. I wouldn't have done that to Mackenzie, would I have? No matter how drunk I might be, or how stupid I'd been acting, I wouldn't have thrown everything away like that. Not for one night of sex with a random girl.

I couldn't have.

"I...I don't know. But it doesn't matter, really, what I think. It doesn't change that you're not happy with what I can give you." She locked eyes with me. "It's time to give up, Austin. I lost, because I couldn't make this work."

"That's not true," I said, my voice cracking on the last word. I pinched the bridge of my nose and took a deep breath. My mind was all foggy right now, and I couldn't think straight. "You're the best thing that's ever happened to me, and we both know it. If there's anyone at fault here, it's me. Not you."

She straightened her spine. "No matter *who* is at fault, you need to accept that things have changed. We can't go back to the way we were."

I nodded. The pain pills had hit my head, and the room spun a little. She had a bit of a halo around her that made her look even more angelic than usual. "I can deal with things changing and not being able to pretend it never happened. But I won't stop reminding you of all the reasons we *do* work. Like how hard we make each other laugh. And how we are two halves that fit together into one perfect piece, and we both know it. And despite what I've done, you can always, *always*, trust me not to spill your secrets—good or bad. No matter what happens to us."

I snagged her hand and tugged her down to the couch. I half expected her to fight me, but she sat at my side, facing me. And she didn't wriggle her hand free.

If anything, she held on to me tighter.

She looked so strong, sitting there with tears in her green eyes, her pink, desirable mouth pressed into a thin line, and her back ramrod straight. "Austin…"

I forced a smile. "Ah, and when you say my name? I swear I hear angels singing. And when you smile, your eyes light up, and it makes me think I can do anything, be anything, and the world is at my fingertips…because of you. You showed me so much, Mac. So damn much, and you don't even know it."

Curling a hand behind her nape, I urged her closer, silently begging her not to reject me. Her lids drifted shut, and she followed my lead. Before a few hours ago, it had been so fucking long since I'd tasted those lips. Felt her skin against mine. Lost myself in her arms. I was like an addict, aching for his next hit.

I needed it *now*.

Our lips touched, and she melted against me, all soft and supple and needy. And, shit, I needed her too. More than she'd ever realize. I yanked her on top of me, my lips moving over hers the whole time. She rested her hand on my chest, fisting my T-shirt, and moaned into my mouth.

We made perfect sense, she and I. We fit together and made each other better. She made me better more than I improved her, but still. We were good for each other, and I'd never make the same rookie mistake I'd made before by opening up to someone over a bottle of Jack. Or getting drunk in public again.

Even though most of that night was still a blur, I knew one thing for sure—I hadn't cheated on my girl. No matter how worried I might be about shit, I had to believe I wouldn't have done that to her. *I had to.*

If she ever doubted anything in this world, she shouldn't doubt this.

Us.

She pulled back, and I groaned, my fingers flexing in her hair. "Mac…please. I need you. I need you so damn much. Don't pull away."

"But—"

"I know I fucked up, and I know we have to deal with it. But tonight, just tonight, can we remember how much we love each other?" I ran my thumb over her lower lip. It was moist and swollen from my kisses. "Can you let me love you?"

For a second, I thought she'd pull away. I even felt her start to. But then she stopped, her eyes locked on mine. This close, I could see the tiny gold flecks that no one else saw. I could see everything she was feeling because of me, because of what I'd done, and it scared the hell out of me.

So I kissed her again, and I prayed like hell she wouldn't pull away, because if she did, then we were over. Completely, utterly *over*.

And I couldn't handle that.

CHAPTER
Seven

Mackenzie

As his lips met mine, I closed my eyes and shut off my mind. Yes, I was doing the "right" thing by letting him go. But, God, I wanted one more time in his arms. One more time where I knew we were good, and we worked, before reality set back in. Before I let him go forever. So I shut my mind off and just *felt*.

And I felt so much.

Pain. Love. Sadness. Desire. It all intermingled into that one kiss, and it almost did me in. Almost sent me running for my room again, but I needed him as much as he needed me. Especially since I knew this would be our last time together. Tomorrow, the news would hit, and we'd be done. Officially. But tonight…

We were together, and we could *be* together one last time. I'd already told him we were over, but I didn't think he'd

LOSING *Us*

accepted it. He thought this was just about him being drunk and stupid, and it was partly because of that. But it was also bigger.

Much bigger than he realized.

Breaking off the kiss, I framed his face and sucked in a gulp of air. My head was spinning. "You realize this doesn't mean we're okay, right? I still stand by what I said earlier."

"I know, I know," he said, smoothing my hair off my face. "So do I."

He closed the distance between us, his mouth touching mine again, and I finally let go of all the pain and fear. Shutting my eyes, I slipped my tongue in between his lips. He tasted as good as I remembered, like man and that unique flavor of Austin. My fingers tightened on his face, and I straddled him, groaning when his hard erection pressed against my core right where I needed him most.

"Shit, Mac, I missed you so damn much," he breathed against my lips.

I nodded, not trusting myself to speak. Kissing him was making me feel better, but it was also making it harder in so many ways. Tears stung my eyes for what had to be the millionth time tonight, but I forced them back. Refused to let them out.

Austin's lips hesitated under mine, as if he knew how much this was hurting me, but I deepened the kiss. His hands lowered to hold my thighs, and he dug his fingers in as he arched his hips up. Pleasure rocked through me—the kind of pleasure only he had given me—and I moaned. With trembling hands, he grabbed my shirt and hauled it over my head. I lifted my arms and broke off the kiss long enough for him to tug it over my head, and then I did the same to his.

When I grabbed his waistband and undid the button, he caught my hands with his own. "Are you sure?" he asked, those bright blue eyes of his pinning me down.

I nodded, not speaking again.

He let go of me, and I undid them, rolling them off his legs and tossing them on the floor. Standing up, I shimmied out of my pants and underwear, not wasting any time. I shrugged off my bra and stood there naked in front of him.

His dark blue eyes flashed with heat. "Come to me. *Now*."

Obeying without a word, I climbed onto the couch and cupped his erection through his black formfitting boxer briefs. He was so hard and big under my palm. His tight abs—and the six-pack I'd never forget, no matter how many years passed—jerked with my touch, and his square jaw flexed.

When I nipped the spot directly over his erection, right above the waistband of his boxers, he hissed and buried his hands in my hair. "Jesus. Mac—"

"Shh." I climbed over his legs, sliding my skin against his. God, I'd missed this. Missed him. And I was going to miss us so much that it just might kill me. "Let me."

His fingers tightened on my hair, but then he relaxed and sagged against the pillows. Taking that as a yes, I rolled off the last piece of his clothing and lowered my head to the tip of his shaft. Closing my eyes, I flicked my tongue over him. He tasted so freaking good, and I knew this was what I needed to do.

I needed to have him, all of him, one more time.

One *last* time.

Closing my mouth around him, I slowly covered his erection with my mouth, swirling my tongue as I descended. A burst of curses exploded out of him, and he urged me closer. Deeper. Opening my mouth, I took more of him in. All of him. He cried out and pumped his hips up once, gently, and I rolled my tongue over him. I sucked harder, scraping my teeth against the head once as I pulled off. Moaning deep in my throat, I slammed back down, my fingers working over his balls as I did so.

After all, I knew *exactly* how he liked it.

"Fuck, Mac," he said, breathing erratically. "Enough."

Without warning, he yanked me up by the hips, lifted me in the air, and lowered me on his face. I barely had enough time to gasp, or to process the fact that I was straddling his head,

LOSING *Us*

before he was moving his tongue over me. I grabbed hold of the couch arm, digging my nails in, and curved my back.

Slowly, I moved my hips against him, losing myself in his magical touch. And when he slapped the side of my ass gently, just like I liked it, I closed my eyes as the orgasm took me by storm. It had been so long, too long, and my body had been more than ready. He flicked his tongue over me one more time, sending me skittering over the edge again. I almost collapsed against the couch, but I wasn't done yet.

And neither was he.

He lifted me again, as if I weighed nothing, and set me down at his hips. I moved my legs, folding them behind me and on top of his thighs, and positioned myself right above his hard length. As I moved him where he needed to be, I rubbed my already sensitive clit against the tip of his penis, and I came again, harder than before.

"*Austin.*"

He groaned and as soon as I had him positioned at my entry, he thrust his hips up, hard, and entered me fully. I cried out, digging my nails into his chest, and tossed my head back. My hair trailed over his thighs and mine, and I rode him with a desperation I'd almost forgotten I could feel. I lost myself in the pleasure, and the need for *more* pleasure. But, beneath it all, was the fact that I was losing this.

Losing us.

"*Mac.*" He fisted my hair and tugged me down so our lips met. "I love you, Mac. I love you so damn much. I love you, I love you, I love you."

I nodded, closing my eyes. Looking at him hurt too much. "I love you too."

Because I did, with all my heart.

As if he'd needed to hear that, he finally seemed to lose control. Rolling me beneath him, he lowered himself over me, cupping my face in his hands, kissed me, and pumped his hips hard and fast. His movements were harsh and hard, but his touch was gentle. Loving. I clung to him for dear life, for more than one reason, and kissed him back. I could feel the pressure building again, hard and fast, and knew it would only be a matter of time until he made me come again.

He always did.

Breaking off the kiss, he lowered his head and bit down on my shoulder, just hard enough to sting. The mixture of pleasure and pain exploded within me, and I went with it. Crying out, I bowed my back and came, stars exploding before my closed eyes.

He moved inside of me once, twice, and then one last time. As he came, my name escaped his lips, and it sounded like a prayer. "*Mackenzie.*"

I buried my face in his shoulder and closed my eyes, letting my heart settle back into a normal rhythm. He cradled me close, his weight still on me but not heavily, and kissed my temple. And then he did it again. I felt so cherished and safe, which was ridiculous because I was neither one. Not anymore. I memorized every single second of this moment, because soon…

It would all be gone.

CHAPTER Eight

Austin

The next morning, I woke up slowly. After our lovemaking session last night, she'd fallen asleep on the couch, with me still inside her. I'd carried her upstairs and laid her on her bed after pulling off her. She hadn't even stirred. For a while, I'd stood there, watching her sleep. Savoring the moment.

Something deep in the pit of my stomach said that we were done, and she'd never forgive me, but the stupid, hopeful, optimistic part of me argued. We loved each other, and we would get through this. We had to, damn it.

I didn't know which part of me was right.

Not anymore.

Turning away because it had hurt too much to look at her anymore, I'd gone downstairs, blown out all the candles, and carefully made my way back upstairs to her bedroom. Part of me had been scared that she would wake up and tell me to find another room, but I'd climbed into her bed, and she hadn't stirred.

We'd slept wrapped in each other's arms for the first time in longer than I could remember, and I'd slept more soundly than I had in months.

Because I'd had her.

In the light of day, that stupid, optimistic part of me came back to life. After last night, and what we'd shared, I was even more certain we could work through this. I'd be fine taking what she could give me, as long as she promised to give me all of her when she did come home.

Even if that was only once a fucking year, I'd make it work, because I loved her. And, more than that, I *needed* her. I didn't want to live a life where she wasn't in it. I'd spent our whole time together trying to be the man who deserved to be at her side. The type of man who had fame and money and was okay with it all.

Hell, I'd never been that guy, and I never would be. I didn't even want to be famous. I'd only done everything I'd done to be good enough for her.

And I'd failed.

Opening my eyes, I blinked up at the white ceiling above her bed. Her comforter was pink, and the canopy curtains that draped over all four posts matched. Her white dressers had crystal knobs on them, and there were picture frames all over the room. Her deceased father. Me. Rachel. We were all there.

It was so very Mackenzie that I couldn't help but smile.

She was still asleep, curled up against me with her head on my shoulder. Her hand rested over my heart, and I smiled even wider. Even in sleep, she knew it belonged to her.

Even if she didn't think she knew it.

My phone vibrated on the nightstand, and I tensed. If it was that Diane girl texting me again, I'd fucking flip my shit. I didn't know what I said to lead that girl on that night in the bar, but she needed to listen to the *last* thing I'd said to her, which was to leave me the hell alone or else.

LOSING *Us*

Being careful not to awaken Mac, I reached out and grabbed my phone. My fingers closed around it as it vibrated again. Jesus, what the hell was going on that I was getting a million notifications at seven in the morning? Blinking, I held the phone in front of my face and scanned the texts from at least six people.

Once the words sank in, my heart froze over...and then blinding pain pounded through the ice from the force of its increased beating. I had tons of messages, and they were all concerning the same damn thing. Something no one else should know about.

Are you okay? Sorry things didn't work out with Mackenzie.
You and Mackenzie broke up?
ARE YOU OKAY?

How the hell did everyone know we'd gotten in a fight? And we hadn't broken up, not yet. Hell, we were naked in bed together right now. And then it hit me...

Diane had told everyone.

That had to be it.

And Mac was going to kill me when she found out. The rumors might become reality if I didn't do something to fix this. She stirred beside me, and I cursed under my breath. I wasn't being given any time to come up with a plan.

As soon as those green eyes focused on me, I started talking fast. "I'm sorry, but someone told the press about our fight. And the whole world thinks we broke up."

She paled and pushed herself up, holding the sheet to her bare chest. "Austin—"

"I know what you're thinking. You're thinking it was Diane, and you're probably accurate in that assumption, and you have every right to be even more pissed at me than you already are." I tossed my phone aside. "Another thing for me to be sorry for, I guess."

Biting down on her lip, she shook her head. Her hair was a frizzy mess, and it was adorable. I loved how soft she looked when she woke up. Like an angel, come to earth. "Austin—"

I sat up, like she had. "I'll call the media and release a statement to fix this. Let them all know that this is some big misunderstanding."

"But it's not." She twisted the sheet in her fists. "There's nothing to fix."

"And I'll—" I stopped midsentence, a cold rush of dread filling my veins. "Wait, what?"

Her lids lowered, she whispered, "I did it. I told them."

I reared back, unable to believe she was saying this. Doing this. "But last night…we…you *told* them?"

"I did." She lifted her chin, staring me down. I felt almost two feet tall. "I told you yesterday that we were done. I thought you understood—"

"Hell no, I didn't understand." I tossed the covers back and lurched out of bed, a sick feeling in my stomach. "We fucking made love last night. That doesn't exactly scream that you don't love me anymore."

"I never said that," she said quickly, two rosy spots on her cheeks. "*Never*."

"Well, you're breaking up with me," I snapped, dragging my hands through my hair. I bumped my sore head, and I flinched, but otherwise ignored it. It was nothing compared to the pain in my heart. "That pretty much says it for you."

She shook her head. "That's not true."

"Jesus, Mac." I covered my face and took a steady breath, trying to make sense of all the emotions crashing through me. "Why? Because I fucked up *one night* and didn't keep my mouth shut when I should have?"

Her shoulders sagged. "No. That's not the only reason."

"Then *why*?"

She stared down at her lap. "Because that's the way you feel. You don't want to be with me anymore, because I can't give you more. You just don't want to admit it out loud to yourself, or me."

I let out a strangled groan. "We went over this last night. I know you're busy, and I'm okay with that."

LOSING *Us*

"No, you're not!" she said, her even tone finally cracking as she raised her voice to me. Good. She should be yelling—and so should I. If we fought, maybe we could actually fix this mess. "And you wouldn't have…you wouldn't have kissed her *back*. I was there, Austin. I saw it all. Saw her boobs pressed up against you and saw the way your hand rested on her back, not pushing her away."

"No." I shook my head. "I didn't want her to kiss me."

She stared me down. "Yeah. You did. You didn't move away, and you kissed her back. Held her for a second. I saw it. You're not happy with me, Austin. Just admit it."

I glowered at her. I hadn't kissed Diane back. Yes, I'd been slow to push her away, but only because a shirtless girl had thrown herself at me in my own dressing room. Of course I froze. I wasn't used to this shit yet, and I didn't like it. "Before I woke up to the news that my girlfriend dumped me, I was *fine*."

"If you were fine, you wouldn't have told that girl you wished you could be free, and that you wanted to be able to enjoy your new life as a hot rock star." She air quoted *hot rock star* with her fingers. "Your words, not mine."

I stiffened. "Bullshit. I didn't say those things."

"You did. It's in the article."

Throwing my hands up, I paced back and forth. "Oh, yes, because we both know how reliable *magazines* are in reporting our personal feelings."

"This particular one? Yes."

"Why?" I asked, stopping in front of her.

Blinking, she lifted her gaze to mine slowly. "It's the one that Diane sold. Everything else in it is stuff you said, so I believe you said these things too."

I swallowed back my automatic protests. I kind of, sort of remembered saying something like that, now that I thought of it. But if I had, then it had been the ramblings of a drunken man. "Even if I did, it didn't mean anything. I was drunk."

She got out of the bed and walked over to her bag,

gloriously naked. Any other day, I'd have admired the view, but not today. Not now. There was too much at stake.

"So you keep saying. But that doesn't make it any less true." Reaching into her bag, she pulled out a magazine and flipped it open. "'Rock star Austin Murphy—'"

"Don't." I crossed the room. "Don't you dare read that shit to me."

She jutted her chin out stubbornly. "'Rock star Austin Murphy wants to spread his wings. Our source says he was spotted cozying up to a hot blonde in a bar down in Florida, while his country sweetheart Mackenzie Forbes tours the world alone. He's quoted to have said, 'I'm sick of always being alone. I miss her, and I miss being able to do what I want, when I want. Hell, I'm a rock star, but I haven't been laid in months.' End quote." She threw the magazine at me, and I caught it out of reflex when it hit my chest. "There's more, but I'll let you read it for yourself. Maybe it'll jog your memory."

I stared down at the magazine, my eyes locked on the picture of Mac and me smiling, with a jagged line drawn through it by the press. "I was drunk."

"I know." She shrugged into a pink robe. "But you still said it, and you meant it. Just *admit* it."

"I didn't cheat on you, and I didn't want to. I—"

She snarled. "*Just admit it!* You wanted to fuck her!"

"So what if I did?" I shouted back. "I didn't, did I?"

"Are you so sure about that?" she asked, her whole body harder than stone. "You were drunk off your ass, as you said. You could have fucked her and forgotten."

"No." I shook my head so hard my ears rang. "I couldn't. Wouldn't."

She stepped closer, her green eyes practically begging me to be sure. To know I hadn't done that to us. "Deep down, to the bottom of your very soul, are you so sure?"

I shook my head again, slower this time, and the doubt she was bringing back to life within me again hit the bottom of my stomach like a brick. Doubt in myself. Doubt I couldn't seem to shake. I thought back to that night, to the loneliness I'd been feeling. I had been in a bad place, and had been for a while. It was true.

But I wouldn't have cheated on her, would I have?

I shook my head and opened my mouth, but nothing came out.

She cried out and covered her mouth, tears welling in her eyes but not escaping. "Oh my God."

"Damn it, I love you, Mac." I covered my face, unable to look at her for another second. "I love you so much."

"No one said you didn't."

"I didn't... I wouldn't have..." I tossed the magazine down. I hadn't even realized I was still holding it till it poked me in the eye. "I have to believe I didn't, because if I did, then I'm a monster. I have to believe—*hope*—that I wouldn't do that to you."

"Your hope isn't enough." Her chin trembled, but she flared her nostrils and lifted her face to mine. Still, no tears escaped. In fact, they went away. "It's not enough for me, just like I'm not enough for you."

Pain sliced through me. "Mac..."

"It's done. I'm letting you off the hook." She wrapped her arms around herself. "You're free to go fuck whoever you want, without me dragging you down."

"That's not fair," I rasped.

"Maybe it is. Maybe it isn't." She turned her back to me and lifted a dainty shoulder. "Either way, it's over."

On autopilot at this point, I stepped into my jeans. As I tugged my shirt over my head, I swallowed past the throbbing lump in my throat. "This is what you want?"

"I—" She hesitated, her hands gripping the robe she wore for dear life. Her knuckles were white. "Yes. It's what I want. Your love isn't going to be enough this time, Austin."

I nodded once, almost falling over at the pain that sliced through me, ripping me in half, much like that picture in the magazine had cut Mac and me apart. "All right."

A small sound escaped her, and she doubled over. "Okay."

"Mac..." I stepped up behind her, reaching out to touch her, but stopping short of actually doing so. My fingers twitched, but I dropped my empty hand back to my side. "I'm sorry. So fucking sorry."

"I know," she said, her voice breathy and raw. "Just...just go."

I didn't have a car, or a ride, but that didn't stop me from walking out of the room barefoot, down the stairs, and out the door. She wanted me to leave, so I did.

I'd hurt her enough already. I wouldn't make it worse by hanging around, waiting for a fucking cab. As I walked outside, the clouds thundered overhead. It had stopped raining, but I had a feeling it wouldn't last long. And I was right. It didn't.

By the time I reached the bottom of the driveway, the skies opened up. I didn't break stride. I just kept walking, letting the rain wash over me. I wished it were so easy to wash off the pain, the anger, and the utter disappointment I had in myself.

I wished I could slide down the gutter like the water and just disappear. It would be easier than this. Anything would be easier than loving, and losing, Mackenzie Forbes.

Anything.

CHAPTER
Nine

Mackenzie

Thirty-six hours. That's how long it had been since I told Austin to leave, and he'd left. As soon as he'd walked out the door, I'd dissolved into a sobbing, wet, snotty mess on the floor. And I hadn't moved for hours. I'd been so sure that he hadn't cheated on me, but when I'd asked him if he was sure...

He'd looked scared. As if he wasn't sure. And that's when it had really hit me. That's when I'd known, without a doubt, that I'd done the right thing. Austin was not a cheater, so if he'd done that to me, he must have been, without a doubt, as miserable as could be. He'd needed to be free. And I deserved better.

We both did.

But that didn't stop the pain, the betrayal, or the agony. If anything, it made it worse. Once I'd been able to move, I'd struggled to my feet and realized two things: One, he'd left without his shoes. And two: He'd left his phone behind.

At first, I'd thought he was in the house somewhere, waiting for a cab to come. But he hadn't been. He'd been gone. He'd just...*left*. I'd gone outside looking for him, but there were no traces. Any trace there might have been had been washed away by the rain. I'd stood there, getting rained on, and had no idea what to do. He hadn't taken his phone, so he wouldn't be able to call anyone. He'd been injured the night before. He didn't know Nashville. And he was barefoot.

Even worse, I had no way to get to him. To find him.

He was on his own.

I'd gone back inside and sat on the stairs, waiting to see if he'd come back to the house for his stuff. Hours passed, and daytime turned to night. The power had whizzed back on, and I still didn't move. I'd fallen asleep leaning against the banister.

And he hadn't come back.

Now, we were both due to perform at Cracker Jack's, and I didn't even know if he would come. Or if he was okay. The worry was eating me alive. My driver pulled up to the venue, and I sat in the backseat, unable to move. Unable to face the new reality that was my life. Word of our split had stretched wide and far, and the paparazzi had been eating up the story. The only thing they'd been lacking was pictures of Austin and me looking miserable to finish off the story. And after tonight, they'd have that.

If he even bothered to show up.

I'd wanted to back out, but my agent had refused my request. Business was business, and the show must go on. All that bullshit they said to make us work. Well, it had worked. I was here. So were what looked like thousands of cameramen and reporters from every channel and news venue imaginable, just waiting for me to open the car door. When I glanced outside, I swore I even saw Ryan freaking Seacrest. But it was a trick of the eye—just another short dude with spiky hair.

The question was...was *Austin* here?

Pulling out my signature cowboy hat, I placed it low over

LOSING *Us*

my head, smoothed my plaid shirt over my short jean shorts, and took a calm, long, deep breath. Then, before I could chicken out, I plastered a smile on my face and exited the vehicle. I was immediately blinded by tons of cameras flashing at me, and I stumbled back a bit as questions got shouted in my face.

I was used to this type of thing, but I wasn't used to *this*. The ferocity.

"Why did he break up with you?" one man shouted.

"Or did you break up with him?" a woman yelled, shoving a microphone in my face.

"Are you doing okay?" from the left.

"Tell us about what happened!" from the back of the crowd.

Someone came at me, and I cried out, but the strong arm that came around my shoulders was all too familiar—as was his spiced, male scent. *Austin.* "Back off," he warned a cameraman that came a little too close for comfort. "Give us space."

My huge longtime security guard, Harry, stepped in front of me. He glowered at Austin but turned his attention to the paps. "Give Ms. Forbes room, now."

Everyone backed off. Austin kept his arms around me and hurried me inside, placing himself between me and as many cameras as he possibly could. Harry took care of the rest. As soon as we cleared the doors of Cracker Jack's, Austin let go of me.

Harry turned on us. "You. You're not—"

"Welcome anymore." Austin stepped back, his eyes on me. I skimmed him hungrily, taking in every inch and simultaneously looking for any signs of bodily damage. He looked okay, all things considering. And he had shoes on. "I know."

"Austin..." I tugged my hat lower. It was a shield of sorts between him and me. I needed that right now. "Thank you for your help."

He shrugged. "Yeah. Sure thing."

I watched him as he spun around and walked away, his hands jammed into his pockets. Swallowing hard, I looked at Harry and forced a smile. "Hey."

"You doing okay?" he asked, his dark brown eyes warm with concern. He'd been my guard for longer than I could remember, and I truly cared for him. And he cared about me. He'd kind of taken the place of my father after he'd died. "Holding up in the craziness?"

"I'm fine," I said, drawing out the last word. "Don't you worry about me. I'm stronger than a new rope in a storm."

"Oh, I already knew that, Ms. Mackenzie." He patted me on the back as he passed me. "Come on. I'll show you to your room."

Nodding once, I followed him, gripping my bag. I had Austin's things inside it. Even though he hadn't mentioned it, I figured he'd like his stuff back. As I followed Harry, I thought back on Austin's intervention. He'd saved me out there, even though we weren't together anymore, and for some reason that hurt.

And it only made me miss him more.

It had been a day and a half since he'd walked out of my life. Did he miss me? Or did he feel as if a weight had been lifted off his shoulders? Did he feel free? Happy? Relieved? Because I didn't feel any of those things. Not at all.

Harry stopped in front of a door with a pink card that said *Mackenzie*. Next to it, on an identical door to the left, was a blue Post-it that said *Austin*. "Here's yours."

I nodded but didn't take my eyes off Austin's name. I needed to give him his stuff, and now was as good a time as any. If I'd been thinking clearly earlier, I would have given it all to him out in the common area. But I hadn't been, so I hadn't.

I'd been too busy looking at him like a starved prisoner.

Slowly, I walked up to the door and traced the paper, leaning in when I heard him laugh. Was he in there with someone else? Had he moved on already? Even worse, was he in there with *Diane*? I swallowed and listened harder, pressing

LOSING *Us*

my ear up against the thin door. Apparently, I couldn't hear well enough, because I didn't hear him walk up to the door...

And *open* it.

"*Oof.*"

I fell inside ungraciously.

He caught me out of reflex with one arm. The other held a phone to his ear. So, he was alone then. "Shit. I gotta go, okay?"

"You don't have to...*sorry.*"

He hung up, shoved his phone in his pocket, and helped me stand straight. As soon as I was steady, he let go of me. "What were you doing?"

My cheeks went hot. I was about to burst into flames, I was sure of it. "I was about to knock," I said quickly. "That's all."

Harry stepped closer. "That's right. She was about to knock."

I closed my eyes for a second. I appreciated his defense, but right now, I didn't need it. It would only make everything look worse. "Harry, can you wait for me out here? And Austin, could I come in for a second?"

He stepped back, motioning me inside. "Sure."

His tone was so...so...cool. So controlled. He seemed okay, and that hurt, because I wasn't okay at all. I was a hot mess. I walked past him, tugging my hat lower. He shut the door and leaned against it, crossing his arms. His muscles flexed as he did so, showing off that ink I'd loved from the first moment I saw him.

We locked eyes, and I opened my mouth, but I didn't say a word. I couldn't.

He cocked a dark brown brow. "What's up?"

"Y-Your phone." I dug in my purse, my pulse racing full speed ahead. "I have it. You left it at my place when..."

"When I left," he supplied when I didn't finish. He pulled an iPhone out of his pocket. The screen lit up, and I saw his background was a picture of him and Rachel. It used to be him and me. Mine still was. I couldn't bring myself to delete it. "I got a new one, and a new number. It was time to lose some old contacts."

Like me. "O-Oh. Okay." I slid the old phone across the table next to me, my finger lingering on it. I almost wanted to keep it. It was some small part of him I could hold on to. "I have your shoes too…"

He flinched and tugged his hat down. It was black and plain. It looked new. "Yeah. Running off barefoot, in hindsight, was not the best idea I've ever had."

"Speaking of which…" I took his shoes out of my bag and set them down. The only thing left of him in my bag was his hat. "Is it bad?"

He walked past me and sat down on the chair in the room. Lifting his foot, he winced and grabbed a hold of it. "I can barely stand, to be honest. Tonight's gonna be rough…" Lowering his head, he mumbled, "In more ways than one."

"Austin…"

"Don't get that concerned tone in your voice. I know that tone all too fucking well." He collapsed back against the chair. "I'm fine."

Fine. Such an ambiguous term. One I'd used just moments before.

Pressing a hand to my throat, I fingered my necklace. The one he'd given me for Christmas. It had a little music note on it and was white gold. "Good."

"Yeah. Good."

I swallowed hard, standing there awkwardly, staring at him. He stared at his foot, his head lowered. "I wasn't sure you'd come. Or if you were okay."

"I wasn't sure if you'd come." He lifted his head and locked eyes with me. The pain in his blue eyes almost sent me staggering back. But then he blinked, and it was gone. "Or if you were okay."

Closing my eyes, I shook my head once. "Honestly? Not really."

"Yeah." He stood. "Me neither."

We fell silent, watching each other again. As if each of us

LOSING *Us*

waited for the other to crack first. The room was fraught with tension, pain, and regret. So much regret. If he gave me even the slightest indication that he was miserable and wanted me back, I'd launch myself in his arms and hold on tight. And I'd never let go.

But he didn't.

"Oh, and your hat." I pulled it out, handing over my last excuse to be in this room with him. "I washed it, and it's as good as new. No stains."

He reached out with a trembling hand and took it, swallowing hard enough for me to see his Adam's apple bob. Taking off his black hat, he settled his Redskins one over his head. "Thank you. That…it means a lot to me."

"I know," I whispered. "And you're welcome."

He glanced at the black hat, then tossed it at me. "Here. You can have this. Maybe you can try something besides those big country hats every once in a while."

Catching the hat out of reflex, I stared down at it. It probably smelled like him. My grip on it tightened. "I like my big country hats."

"Yeah. I know." His phone rang, and he glanced down at it. When he saw who it was, he frowned. "I have to take this. So…?"

"Right." I nodded and headed for the door, feeling worse than before I'd entered, which was saying a lot. The hat came with me. "See you out there."

"Are we still doing the duet?" he asked, his voice rough.

I froze, my hand on the knob. He referred to the song we'd recorded together. It was a sweet country song, and Austin's voice even held the appropriate amount of twang needed when he sang it. He'd come out at the end of my set, join in, and we'd close out the show together. It had been, up until now, my favorite part of every show.

No. No, no, no, no. "Do you want to?"

He shrugged, looking unconcerned. He'd have looked livelier if we had been discussing the stocks or the weather.

"They'll be watching to see. If we don't, they'll just blast all over the news how horrible we're both dealing with the breakup."

"Then we'll do it." I opened the door and walked out.

He lifted his phone to his ear and said, "Hello?"

As I closed the door, I peeked inside. I was starved of his face, and I needed to see him one last time. He took his hat off and rubbed his forehead, the mask he'd worn around me dropping. And what I saw, the stark exhaustion and pain in his face, almost sent me running back inside that room.

But I closed the door instead.

CHAPTER Ten

Austin

Mackenzie was trying to kill me. Okay, she might not be trying...but she was. She really was. I was barely holding my shit together, and she was out there giving the performance of her career. She was okay, and I was a hot fucking mess.

How was that fair?

How was *any* of this fair?

My phone buzzed in my hand, and I glanced down at it. Barry, the owner of the bar I worked and performed at, was calling. He'd kind of been the father I'd never had, since I didn't count my actual father. He'd been a dick, and nothing more.

Barry had been so much more.

Gripping my phone, I turned my back to the stage and Mackenzie, who I couldn't stop watching even though it hurt like hell, and walked behind a big speaker. My heart thudded in my ears, washing out Mackenzie's song. I was sitting by the side stage, waiting for my cue to come on with her. It should be any minute now.

"Hello?"

"Hey, you called?" Barry asked. I could hear the bar noises behind him, and it made me homesick. "Sorry, was working in the cooler."

"Yeah. I had a question."

I tried to think of the best way to phrase it…and apparently took too long. After a little pause, Barry said, "And it was…?"

"The other night, I came in with a girl."

"I remember," Barry said, his voice deep with disappointment. "I told you that you were being a fool. You laughed and walked off, like the cocky son of a bitch you are."

"I should have listened," I muttered.

"When do you ever listen?" Barry asked, his voice tinged with amusement.

"Did I… Did I do anything… Did I…?"

"No. Absolutely not."

I sagged against the wall, my heart pounding in my chest. "Are you sure? One hundred percent positive?"

"Yes, of course." He snorted. "Do you think I'd let you do something so stupid as to cheat on that sweet little girl? Who do you think I am?"

I closed my eyes, the nausea that had been plaguing me since yesterday sinking low in my stomach and dissipating. "How do you know, though? She could have come over to my place once I went home."

"No, she couldn't have. I walked you home and crashed on your couch, in case you got sick." Glasses clanked, and he muttered something to someone. "I knew Rachel was at a friend's house, so I didn't want you to die in a puddle of vomit or something. You might be a rock star now, but doesn't mean it's gotta end like that. You were never alone with that girl, as much as she might have hoped otherwise."

"Oh thank fucking God. I could kiss you right now."

"Why would you think you did anything, anyway?" Barry

closed a door behind him. Probably his office door, considering how much quieter the background noise got. "You love Mac, right?"

"I know, but..." I rubbed my forehead. "I said some stupid things that night, and she...she broke up with me. And since I'd said those things, I'd worried that maybe I'd done more than talk. That I'd been a monster."

Like father, like son.

Barry sighed. "Nah. You just blubbered on like a drunk fool. I don't know how you got so drunk and slurred so fast, to be honest. You didn't have *that* much."

I dropped my head back against the speaker. Closing my eyes, I fought the urge to kick myself in the nuts. "I don't know, man. All I know is I don't remember saying any of that stuff, except in bits and pieces. I was really fucked up from what I can piece together."

"Tell her you love her and can't live without her, and tell her you're sorry." Barry sighed. "That always works, man."

"I tried all of that. It didn't change a damn thing." I turned around and watched her on stage. She was on her game tonight, as if nothing had happened to us. It only proved... "She's done."

"But—"

She started her last song before I came out, so I cut him off. "Look, I have to go. I'm almost up. Thanks, man, for letting me know I slept alone that night."

"You're welcome. But you should tell—"

I hung up on him, my jaw tight. I didn't need to tell her anything. I'd done what I'd done, ruined what I'd ruined, and it was over. I just had to get through tonight, and then I could move on and try to pick up the pieces of my life.

Without her.

I walked toward the side stage again, my whole body screaming out in protest. Everything hurt. My feet. My legs. My arms. My head. And worst of all...my heart. My heart hurt so fucking bad that I'd consider offering it to science just to make it stop.

It wasn't just the physical pain I was in, because I was. A lot. But it was the fact that if I went out there on that stage and sang with her about love…

A small part of me might die.

By the time I'd finished my set earlier, I'd been more relieved to get off the stage than ever before, and I didn't want to go back on. Girls had yelled up to me how I was single now, and they were, too, and it made me sick. I didn't want to be single, damn it.

I wanted Mackenzie.

But she didn't want me. Not anymore.

All because I'd been a dumbass who'd made a silly, stupid, horrible mistake that had cost me everything. If I hadn't gotten wasted, you could damn well bet none of this would've happened. I'd never had said those stupid things to some girl in a bar, Mac wouldn't have read the article, and Diane wouldn't have felt welcomed enough to wait for me in my dressing room topless.

I leaned against the speakers and watched Mac sing, my heart somehow beating rapidly in my chest after all it had been through. She danced around the stage, singing her heart out, and if I didn't know any better, I'd say she was perfectly happy.

Hell, maybe she was.

She'd said she was breaking it off with me for *me*, but what if she was doing it for *her*? What if she'd been the one who wanted to be free, and she'd just used my drunken escapades as an excuse to get it? I stiffened, watching her closer.

Maybe her act wasn't an act at all.

Perhaps she was fucking fine, unlike me. She kicked her leg up and danced across the stage, belting out her tune about dancing all night long to her own song. It had a fun, wild, free beat to it. Maybe she'd picked it for a reason.

Maybe I was the only miserable one here.

After walking for a few miles with bare feet, across wet pavement and jagged rocks, I'd pretty much thought I hit rock bottom. But then I'd stumbled into a bar, gotten drunk, and called a cab…and realized I had nowhere to go. I was barefoot, phoneless, girlfriendless, and I'd lost Mac.

That had been rock bottom.

It had been when I realized I'd ruined every good thing in my life. I still had Rachel, yes, but eventually she'd go off to college. Start a great career. Get married and have kids. And I'd be the loser brother she invited over for Christmas.

I was *that* guy.

After sleeping off the massive hangover I'd gotten from my little drinking binge, I'd gone out, gotten clothes and shoes, a new phone with a new phone number so Diane didn't have my contact info anymore, and tried to straighten my shit up.

But damn it, I *missed* her.

She ended her song with a high kick and a yell, grinning when everyone cheered her on. Bowing, she took her hat off and tossed it into the crowd like she always did at the end of a show. I hated those damn hats, so I liked when she got rid of them.

Some teenaged girl caught it, hugging it to her chest and crying. I'd have the same reaction if Mac looked at me right now and told me she loved me.

She *did* look at me, but simply to signal me to come out when she finished her speech. I nodded to her once and straightened my green shirt over my stomach. Stepping up to the mic, she tapped her fingers on the side nervously and pulled it out of the stand. As she sat down on one of the two stools that had been placed on the stage as Mac threw her hat into the crowd, she shook her knee uneasily.

Her mic was covered in jewels. Mine, like usual, was plain black. My stool was directly next to hers. So close that our legs would touch.

"So, as you all know, Austin Murphy is here with me." The crowd went wild, and she paused, letting them. Once they quieted, she smiled and nodded. "I know, right? But he's here, and we're going to sing our song that will be on both of our upcoming albums. Give him a warm, happy Tennessee welcome."

The crowd went wild, and I stepped out, waving and smiling as I went. As I walked up to Mac, I nodded at her once, tugged my hat down, and pulled my mic out.

Time to sing the song that talked about how strong our love was, and how we'd never give up on one another. When we'd recorded this song, we'd been so happy. So in love, and so together, and now we were neither of those things.

It felt wrong to sing it while feeling this way, but I'd do it for her.

Anything for her.

"Thank you, everyone. And thank you, Mackenzie." I cleared my throat and sat down. My guitar sat in a stand against my stool, but I didn't pick it up. I couldn't look away from her. She watched me with those green eyes that were so bright under the lights that it hurt to see them, so I looked away. "You ready to hear our song 'All In'?"

They cheered, and I picked up my guitar, slinging it over my shoulder. As I strummed the first chords, Mac straightened her back and tapped her foot to the beat.

The show must go on, after all.

As I hit the end of the last chord, I nodded, and we both started singing right on cue.

You, my love,
Are my love.
When I saw you, that night,
I gave in to you without a fight.
And I know why, now.
Yes, I know why.
Without you, the world is black.
With you, I never wanna go back.
Oh, no, I never wanna go back.
Like a game of cards, baby.
I'm all in, my love.

LOSING Us

I'm all in.

As we finished that verse, I glanced over at her to make sure we were still okay with the rhythm. After I did, I wished I hadn't. Tears streamed down her face, and I almost threw the guitar aside and hugged her, but I kept playing. And we kept singing.

Every. Fucking. Word.

By the time we reached the end, the crowd was silent and cameras were snapping pictures. It wasn't until I swiped a forearm across my cheek that I realized they were wet. Hell, had I been crying too? I didn't fucking cry.

Shit, I hadn't cried since the night my dad had tried to kill my baby sister.

I didn't think I even knew how. Not really. Standing up, I let my guitar hit the stage with a loud crash and stormed off without looking at Mac or the crowd. The whole time I walked, flashes went off without mercy. This was going to be all over Twitter within seconds. *Fuck, fuck, fuck.* If she saw me…if she knew…

I'd fucking die.

I heard Mac say a few quick words, and then heard her footsteps behind me. I hurried my steps, refusing to turn around. Refusing to let her see my shame.

"Austin!"

I shook my head and swiped my hands across my cheeks, removing any evidence of my weakness. It hurt too much to hear her voice. To know she was behind me. To know she'd seen me at my frailest. "Go away, Mac. Just *go away*."

"But—"

"Damn it, Mac," I growled. Spinning around, I trapped her against the wall, kissing her with all the pain, anger, and disappointment I felt right now—which was a hell of a lot. She pushed at my shoulders for a brief second, then curled her hands in my shirt and pulled me closer. Our tears mingled until I didn't know whose were whose.

But it didn't matter.

By the time I pulled back, her sweet taste forever emblazoned upon my brain, I was fucking lost. More so than ever before. I didn't know what to do in a world with no Mackenzie Forbes. But I let go of her anyway, because I didn't really have a choice. Not anymore. "I had to do that one last time before I walk away for good. I can't be around you anymore. I can't be there, singing with you, and be okay with it. I just can't."

She bit down on her lower lip. "I can't either."

"Then it's settled. No more duets. No more shows. No more...anything."

Closing her eyes, she wrapped her arms around herself. "This was the last one we had scheduled publicly. Your gig in Florida didn't have my name on it, officially."

"Right." It had been our planned surprise for the local crowd, an impromptu show together at Captain Crow's. I swallowed hard, dipping my head so she couldn't see my face. I didn't want her to see me right now. Hell, she'd never see me again, really. "So it's done."

"I can take the song off my album." She hesitated. "If you don't want me to use it anymore."

"I don't give a damn what you do with the fucking song."

She flinched. "Okay."

"I didn't fuck her. For what it's worth. Barry told me I went home alone, and he took me there. I went to bed, and he tucked me in. Stayed the night with me." I swallowed hard. "I just wanted you to know that."

Without waiting for a reply, I turned and walked away. *Again*.

No, for the last time.

CHAPTER
Eleven

Mackenzie

The next morning, my plane landed in Florida at six o'clock, and I still hadn't slept a wink in a bed for more than a day and a half. I couldn't sleep. Couldn't eat. I was a mess, and nothing was making it any better. I'd been ten seconds from cancelling my spring break trip with Cassie and Quinn, but truth be told?

I needed my girls.

If anyone could pull me out of this slump, it was them. We'd just have to avoid Cherry Street and Captain Crow's. And anything that reminded me of Austin.

So, basically, everything.

As I walked off the plane, all bleary eyed and frizzy haired, I tugged the black baseball hat Austin had given me lower over my head. I didn't usually wear them, but I wanted to blend in. And it smelled like him just the tiniest bit, even though he'd only worn it for a day or so. Pathetic? Maybe.

But I was past caring.

As I walked with my head down, I hurried to the baggage claim and stood there, tapping my foot impatiently and stifling a yawn. I'd left before the butt crack of dawn to avoid running into Austin because I knew his flight left at ten in the morning…since I'd been planning on flying home with him. No way in hell that was happening now.

I didn't fuck her. For what it's worth.

His voice echoed in my head for the millionth time. He hadn't cheated on me, and that made the pain a little bit less. But he'd still said, and meant, those things. And he'd wanted to be free, right? He hadn't given me a reason to think otherwise. Last night at the concert, he'd sung that song with me without breaking stride even a little bit. I'd been a sobbing mess and too scared to look at him in case he noticed.

But he'd stayed cool right through the end.

Laughter sounded from behind me, all too familiar laughter, and I stiffened. *No*. It couldn't be him. He wasn't even supposed to be here till later this afternoon.

"You're so much hotter in person," a girl simpered. "Can we get a picture together? Please?"

"Sure," Austin said, his voice polite and deep. "Real quick."

I heard them shuffle, and then a camera snapped. "Thank you so much! I love you, seriously. I love you."

Austin chuckled, the sound sexy and deep without him even trying. And the girl was eating it up, judging from the giggles I heard behind me. "I love you, too, Ms. …"

"Rebecca! My name's Rebecca." She giggled again. "Wow, your arms are hard. Like, *so hard*."

"Thanks. I'm—" He broke off, and I knew, I just *knew*, he'd spotted me. "Happy to meet you. Have a nice trip, Rebecca."

"I'll come see you in Captain Crow's this weekend," she called out.

"Great, see you then," he said, his voice distracted. I heard his footsteps approach, and I closed my eyes, silently begging

God to make him not see me. For him to have—

"What are you doing here, now?"

My shoulders sagged, and I clung to my purse as if it were a life vest. "Probably the same thing you are—avoiding our flight home together."

"Shit." He stood beside me and crossed his arms. He had bags under his eyes, and he looked as exhausted as I felt. "Figures."

"Yeah..."

He rocked back on his heels and let out a sigh. "You're wearing the hat?"

"Yeah. I was trying to blend in." I tapped my fingers on my purse, willing my cheeks to cool it. "It must've worked, since we flew on the same plane and didn't even notice one another."

"I was in coach," he said.

"I wasn't." I swallowed. It hurt. "But I boarded late, so you wouldn't have seen me when you passed. Almost missed the flight."

As soon as the words were out of my mouth, I rolled my eyes internally. This had to be the most forced conversation *ever*. We'd both tried to avoid one another, and failed miserably. And now here we were, standing next to each other, waiting for our bags, sharing idle chat. What had I done to piss off the big guy in the sky so horribly?

He cleared his throat. "To be honest, I didn't think you'd come back here since we're not doing that show together anymore."

"Yeah, well." I licked my parched lips. "I had to. I'm meeting Cassie and Quinn here for spring break, and I wanted to...I don't know. Enjoy the warmth for a while. Stupid, I know. I should have just stayed in Nashville."

"Ah, that's right," he said, a small frown slipping over his face. "I'd forgotten they were coming down. Guess they'll hate me again, huh?"

Shrugging, I looked at the screen. *When* was the freaking luggage going to come out? "I have no idea. I don't tell them how they should feel about other people."

"No, you only do that to me."

I winced but remained quiet.

He clucked his tongue and then turned on me. Even though I could feel his gaze burning into me, I didn't look at him. "You look like you haven't been sleeping."

I closed my eyes again, my cheeks heating. "In other words, I look like shit."

"I didn't say that," he argued. "Don't put words in my mouth again. You've done that enough, thank you very much."

I pressed my lips together. "Is that some sort of dig, or what?"

"What do you think?" he asked, his tone almost…bored.

"I don't know," I snapped. "If I did, I wouldn't have asked."

He took off his hat, dragged his hand through his hair, and then slammed it back down. The spot where he'd hit his head on my stairs was still bruised and scabbed over, but it didn't seem to bother him anymore. "I read that article, by the way. None of that shit you read were my actual feelings on the matter…not that you care."

I whirled on him. "Stop it."

"Stop what? Being pissed at you? At myself? At this whole fucking situation?" He stepped in my personal space, his hands curled into balls, and glared down at me. "Because I'm so fucking pissed, Mac, you wouldn't believe it. You have no idea."

I forced myself not to step back from him. "You didn't sound pissed while you were flirting with *Rebecca*."

"Oh my God, you—" The carousel started with three loud beeps, and he broke off, shaking himself. "You know what? Fuck it. I don't need to explain myself to you anymore. You saw to that when you told the world that we were split up."

I bit my tongue. I wouldn't fight with him. Wouldn't poke him just to— "What did you think I was going to do? Be thankful that you changed your mind and didn't want to fuck other women after all?"

LOSING Us

He threw his hands up. "I never wanted to fuck other women in the first place, but you won't believe me, will you?"

"No. You admitted to saying it!"

"But I was—" He shook his head. His blue luggage came around the corner, and he grabbed it. "Never mind. I'll leave you alone now."

I grabbed his arm. "Are you denying saying that now?"

"Does it matter?" He yanked free. "Does it really fucking matter at all?"

I swallowed the words trying to escape. "I guess not."

"Exactly." He glanced around, his brow knitted. "Where's Harry?"

"There was only one seat left on the flight," I said hollowly. "He'll be here later."

"So you're alone?"

I nodded once. "I'm a big girl. I can take care of myself."

"Until you walk out that door and the paparazzi sees you. You know they'll be there." My luggage came out, and he sighed and bent down to pick it up. After setting it beside me and extending the handle, he straightened his hat. "I'll go out first and distract them, then you can slip out a few seconds later."

"Thank you, but you don't have to take care of me anymore. I can just—"

"I said that I'll go out first, damn it." He gave me one last long stare. "Goodbye, Mac. I...I...I wish you the best, despite everything that happened."

I swallowed hard and forced a smile. *Come back. Kiss me. Love me. Tell me you need me. I'll believe you, I swear it.* "I wish the same for you. So very much."

He hesitated but left. I watched him go, watching as the crowds converged on him. He tugged on his hat and answered a few questions, and I slipped away unnoticed by all except one. *Austin.* As I settled into my seat, the driver tossed my luggage in the back.

I pulled out my phone. I had more than two hundred

Twitter notifications, three thousand and six unread emails, fifty-two voicemails, and a hundred and fifteen texts. Ignoring them all, I opened up the group message with Cassie and Quinn. *Landed in Florida, staying at the Cove Suites again. See you guys once you get here/are available.*

Are you okay? Quinn asked.

What she said, Cassie typed directly after.

Yes, we'll talk more this week, but I'm fine. I looked out my window, watching as Austin posed for a picture with a gorgeous brunette. She had her hands on his abs, dangerously low. Forcing my eyes off them, I turned my attention back to my phone. To my girls. *I'll be fine after a few drinks, anyway. Hope you guys are having a better week than me.*

Yeah... Cassie said.

Totally... Quinn said.

I shook my head. I'd known that Cassie hadn't been doing well since the breakup with Ty, but what was wrong with Quinn and James now? Why was everything falling apart? *Least convincing texts ever. Looks like we'll all need those drinks.*

Sold! Quinn typed.

It's a deal, Cassie replied.

I winced, feeling my friends' pain through the phone. I wanted them to get here so I could hug them both and tell them how much I appreciated them. Loved them. Needed them.

The driver sat down, closed the door, and smiled at me. "Cove Suites, Ms. Forbes?"

"Yes, please," I said, setting my phone down and looking at Austin once more. He looked toward my car, his hat shadowing his face so I couldn't read his expression. "Thank you."

The car pulled away from the curb, and the last thing I saw was Austin leaning down to whisper something in the brunette's ear, and she grinned. As much as Austin said he didn't want to be free, he looked *awfully* happy to be.

And I'd *so* wanted to be wrong.

CHAPTER Twelve

Austin

Later that night, I wiped the bar off at Captain Crow's and scowled at the crowd. Everyone was laughing and having fun, while I was fucking miserable. I couldn't sleep. Could barely eat. And everyone kept asking me if I was okay.

No, I wasn't fucking okay.

Why would I be?

On top of that, all night long women looking to comfort me mobbed me, and I didn't want their damn comfort. I wanted my Mac back, but that didn't stop them from trying anyway. And I'd had it up to my neck with all this shit.

Before I could so much as blink after sending one girl away, a blonde leaned in, showing off an admittedly impressive display of cleavage. "I'll have an appletini." Behind her, at least three girls waited for their turn. "What time do you get off tonight?"

"I don't know." I handed her the fruity concoction she'd asked for and stepped back. "That'll be eight dollars, miss."

She pulled a ten out of her bra and winked. "Keep the change."

"Gee. Thanks," I said drily, taking the warm bill from her hand.

For some reason, she seemed to take that as a welcome for more flirtation. "Can I have your number?" she asked, biting down on her lip. "I'm in town till Sunday, and you're single now…"

"I don't give my number out. Sorry."

She pouted when I walked away, but I didn't give a damn. I wasn't in the mood to be chivalrous and kind to my fans, if she even was one. Something told me she'd never listened to a second of my music. She'd just jumped on the bandwagon that was…well, *me*, hoping to get laid by a famous guy.

Bragging rights and all that shit.

Unfortunately for her, I wasn't in the frame of mind to oblige.

"Stop glaring at my customers." Barry came up behind me as I put the cash in the drawer and slid a full glass toward me. "You know you don't need to work here anymore, right?"

I caught it out of reflex. "I know, but you needed help."

"Doesn't mean I need you here, scaring everyone away. Not to mention it's bad PR for you." He flung a rag over his shoulder and crossed his arms. "Drink that. It'll help you relax."

"I'm not allowed to drink on the job," I said, frowning down at the glass. "Your rules, not mine."

"Yeah, well, ignore them this one time."

I gripped the edge of the bar and lowered my head. "I don't want a fucking drink. That's what got me where I am in the first place."

"No, being an idiot is what got you there." He cocked his gray head to the side, his brown eyes focused on me. "Are you planning on being an idiot tonight?"

I snorted. "Hell no."

LOSING Us

"Then drink."

Gritting my teeth, I picked up the glass and chugged back the cold Coors. It soothed my throat and my thirst, but I didn't feel any better. Slamming it down on the bar, I narrowed my eyes at Barry. "There. Happy?"

"Nope." He came toward me. "And you won't be, either, until you give yourself time to feel better. You need to go out. Drink. Dance. Flirt with a pretty girl. Forget about that sweet little thing that broke your heart, and be a guy. Maybe find a rebound girl and—"

I shook my head, my heart wrenching sharply to the left. "No. I can't. I'm not ready."

"All right." He tipped his head to the side. "Well, if you change your mind once that beer hits, the brunette in the corner is watching you awfully closely."

I glanced out of habit. Barry was right.

A pretty brunette with soft brown eyes watched me as she sipped her drink. I hadn't served her, so I didn't know what she was drinking, but judging by the way she was chugging it back, she'd soon be out. At least she wasn't throwing herself at me, unlike the rest of the women. "I'm not interested."

"Well, go serve her anyway." Barry eyed the long line of women at the bar. "I'll get them."

I walked over to the brunette, tossed my rag aside, and stopped in front of her. "Need another, ma'am?"

"Oh my God, yes." She slid the glass toward me. "Maybe ten more."

I cocked a brow. "Bad night?"

"Yep. My boyfriend cheated on me, and I have nowhere to go." She squinted at me. "Hey. Anyone ever tell you that you look a lot like Austin Murphy?"

Stiffening, I barely refrained from rolling my eyes. She was going to try and act as if she didn't know who I was, and it only made me miss Mac even more. That trick wouldn't work on me—hell, I'd created that playbook. I'd tried to pretend I hadn't known Mac when we'd met. "All the time. Whatcha drinking?"

"Rum and Coke." She slipped off the barstool and almost fell. "Oops. That was a little too fast for me, I think."

Shaking my head, I didn't get her another drink. "I think you're cut off for the night. I can't serve you if you're visibly drunk."

"But—" She covered her mouth, her eyes wide. "Uh-oh."

"You need to go home before you vomit all over the bar," I said, stepping back warily. The last thing I needed was some random chick's puke all over my Converses. "Let me call you a cab, okay?"

"Okay," she slurred, reaching into her purse and tossing money at me. "I have ten dollars. Will that be enough?"

Probably not. "Yeah. Sure."

Picking up the phone, I called her a cab and nodded to Barry when he raised a brow at me. He came over, leaned in, and whispered, "Please walk her to the cab. I don't want her disappearing out there in a drunken stupor."

"Why did you serve her so much?" I hissed, my eyes on the brunette. She sat at the bar, her head in her hands. "She's fucking wasted and two seconds from blowing."

"I didn't do that to her," Barry said, glaring at me. "She must've been that way when she came, and it hadn't hit yet or something. I only served her once."

I sighed. "I'll start getting her outside. At least if she pukes out there, I don't have to clean it up."

"Thanks. It's almost closing time, so once you see her off you can go home."

To my empty house? No, thank you. "But—"

"Go. Home." He pointed at me. "That's an order, son."

And with that, Barry walked toward the crowd of women staring at me.

"Shit," I muttered under my breath. Rolling my shoulders, I made my way out from behind the bar and over to the brunette. "Your cab will be here soon. Let's get you outside and into the fresh air."

"O...kay." She stood unsteadily, and I caught her before

LOSING *Us*

she hit the floor. "Oops. Sorry 'bout that."

I squared my jaw as a camera flashed the second I touched her. Great. Just fucking great. "I got you. Come on."

She wrapped her arms around me, and I slung mine around her waist, practically holding her up as she stumbled forward. "Thank you," she slurred. "You're, like, my hero or something."

Behind us, even more flashes went off.

This would be all over Twitter in a matter of minutes.

"Easy now," I said when she almost fell out of my arms. "Take it slow."

She paused and rested a hand on my chest, blinking up at me. "Wait a second… You're him, aren't you? I can't be *that* drunk."

"Are you here alone, or do you have friends with you?" I asked, ignoring her question.

"They're in their hotel room. Didn't want to go out with me, so I went alone." She waved a hand dismissively. "Who needs them, anyway?"

She did, obviously.

As she clung to me, I came to the realization I couldn't just dump her in a cab and walk away with a clear conscience. This girl was wasted outta her mind, and she was someone's sister. Someone's daughter. If Rachel got drunk and needed a stranger to help her home…

I'd damn well hope that stranger would help.

Which is exactly why Barry had sent me out with her. He'd known I'd feel bad for her and see her home safely. Damn him. "But they're there, right? Can you call them so they meet us in the lobby?"

She pursed her lips. "Wait. You're coming with me?"

"Just to drop you off. Nothing else." I adjusted my hold on her and eyed the bench outside the bar. We might be waiting a while, and something told me she didn't have much standing power left in her. "Come on, let's sit."

She followed me—not that she had much choice since

I was supporting her—and we sat down. She stayed draped across me, her eyes intently focused on me. Well, as intently as she could be while drunk off her ass. "Are you okay? You look sad."

"That's because I am sad," I admitted, staring up at the stars. They used to soothe me as a kid, back when I'd dream that somewhere out there the world was a happy place. That my happy ending existed. They did nothing for me now. "Just like you."

"Oh."

"Yeah," I said.

We sat in silence as we waited for the cab. Once it came, I settled her into the back and shut the door behind us. "Where are you staying?"

"The Cove Suites," she said.

Of *fucking* course she'd be staying at Mac's hotel. Where the hell else would she be staying? One of the other hundreds of hotels in the city? Nah. Too easy. "You heard her," I said to the driver. "Cove Suites."

He took off, and I leaned against the seat, dragging a hand through my hair. As we pulled out onto the road, I glanced over at the brunette. She rested her head on the window and closed her eyes. "You okay over there?" I asked.

"Yeah. Just sleepy."

"Okay." I rubbed my thighs, looking out the window. We were already more than halfway there. With any luck, I'd have her handed off to her friends before Mac found out I was there. I'd make sure of that. "Did you text your friends that you're on your way to the hotel?"

"Nope. I didn't bring my phone."

Jesus fucking Christ. This girl was trying to kill me. "Do you know their room number?"

"Yeah. Two fifteen."

"Okay." I tapped my foot impatiently and picked up my phone. After calling and getting a hold of one of her friends in their room, I got them to agree to meet us in the lobby. As I hung up, I eyed her nervously. She looked as if she was about to pass out. "They'll be waiting for us once we get there."

She didn't even answer. Just nodded.

Once we got to the hotel, I helped her out of the cab and scanned the lobby through the glass doors. No sign of Mac, so it looked as if the coast was clear. I didn't see Harry, either, so she wasn't there. Good.

Maybe I'd escape before she was.

"Here we go," I said, hauling her out like a rag doll. "Let's go find your friends."

She stumbled into my arms. "Are they there?"

I looked again. I didn't see anyone who looked like her friends. Of fucking course. "Not yet, but let's go in anyway." I walked her inside, and then had the front desk call up to the room again. As we waited I scanned the lobby. The coast was still clear. "Come on."

"Are you him? Are you Austin Murphy?" she asked, her voice soft with wonder.

I glanced down at her and nodded once.

Her eyes went even wider. "Did you and Mackenzie really break up?"

"Yes. We did."

"I'm sorry," she whispered. Her hand on my chest hesitated before she cupped my face. "I can make it better, for both of us."

Before I could even form a reply, she lurched forward and kissed me. Her lips were soft and sweet, but they weren't Mac's. And I hadn't lied before. I wasn't ready. I shook my head and grabbed her hand, pulling back. "I—"

Something hit the floor, and I glanced up with dread. Mac stood there in front of the main doors, her face white and a cup of coffee splattered in front of her feet. Harry was conspicuously absent. At the same time I saw her—and she saw *me* kissing the damn brunette—the elevator doors opened and out came the brunette's friends.

As soon as they saw me, they started screaming and

flailing. When they saw Mackenzie, they screamed even more and whipped out their phones. "Oh my God! It's them!" one of them called out.

"Mac, wait. I can explain—"

"I can't believe you." Mac pressed a trembling hand to her stomach. "You…out of all the hotels in this town…you *asshole*."

With that, she bolted for the elevator. I let go of the drunken brunette and let her slouch against the wall. I rushed after Mac, my heart banging in my chest louder than a freight train. "*Mac*. This isn't what it looks like."

She bolted into the elevator and jammed her finger into her floor button. The doors started to shut, so I threw myself through them with barely a second to spare. I didn't care if they flattened me, damn it, all that mattered was catching up with Mac. As they closed behind us, she pushed me backward. "How dare you? Do you…do you *hate* me that much that you *had* to bring that girl here and kiss her in *my* lobby?"

I held my hands up and shook my head, my stomach twisting in dread. She'd never forgive me for this. Not after what I'd already done. "I didn't kiss her, she kissed me."

"And you just *happened* to be in *my* hotel?"

"Yes!" I said, dragging my hands down my face. "I had to bring her back from the bar because she was drunk. I didn't know she was staying here until we were in the cab."

She waved an arm, her cheeks red. "Well, don't let me stop your drunken conquest. Hey, go out there. Have fun. Fuck some girls. It's what you wanted, right?"

"The hell I did." I stepped toward her, into her personal space, and loomed over her. "All I fucking want is you, but you never believe me."

Letting out a harsh laugh, she glared up at me. "You have a bad way of showing it, if that's the case. Kissing some floozy in my lobby doesn't exactly scream 'I miss you' to me, but maybe I'm the crazy one."

Anger hit me hard, taking away all common sense and all

honorable intentions. I hadn't followed her up here to fight with her, or beg her to take me back. I just hadn't wanted her to think I was fucking that girl when I wasn't. That was all.

But now that had changed.

Narrowing my eyes, I backed her against the elevator wall. "Let me show you the proper way," I said between my clenched teeth. "I'll show you exactly how much I fucking miss you, sweetheart."

And then I pulled her into my arms.

CHAPTER Thirteen

Mackenzie

The second I'd seen him in my lobby, kissing that girl, something inside me had broken into a million pieces. I'd known he would move on, and I'd known he'd be in someone else's arms eventually, but I hadn't wanted to *see* it, for the love of God. And he shouldn't have brought her to the hotel he'd known I would be in.

That had been cruel and unnecessary.

And then, as if that wasn't bad enough, he'd chased after me and tried to excuse his behavior. Tried to tell me he *missed* me. Yeah, sure, that had been completely clear by the way he'd had his tongue in another girl's mouth. Crystal freaking clear.

He backed me against the wall and pulled me close. Some tiny part of me wanted to melt into him, because his arms felt so good around me. But the other louder, bigger part of me was pissed as hell at him.

LOSING *Us*

I hissed out a short breath.

No way. He wasn't going to get his hands on me, not after that little display in the lobby. "Don't even think about it," I said, pressing my hands against his chest and pushing him back. He didn't budge. "I don't do sloppy seconds, or second best."

He flexed his jaw. "You calling me second best now?"

"No, but you obviously think *I* am." I pushed him again and the doors opened. "Go back to your all-too-willing companion and…and…" I swallowed hard. "Leave me the hell alone. You got what you wanted. I saw you with her; now go back to her and finish what you started."

"Sure, I'll get right on that, since I have your permission," he snapped.

I stumbled past him, refusing to cry. Refusing to show him how much he'd hurt me by bringing that girl to the hotel for me to see. Two more steps. That's all I needed before I'd be closed behind my door, safe and sound. Then I could break. Cry. Scream. I could—

"This isn't what I wanted at all," he said from behind me. He'd followed me off the elevator. Great. "None of this is what I *wanted*, damn it."

"Then you shouldn't have come here."

I swiped my card through my lock and opened the door, fully intending to slam the door in his face. He slipped inside before I could, shutting the door behind him.

For the second time in one night.

"I didn't bring her here for you to see, or to fuck her, even. She was at the bar, and I was working. Barry asked me to take her home safely—that's it." He fisted his hands. "She couldn't call her friends because she didn't have her phone, and she didn't have enough money to get home, so I helped her, like a good guy should."

I crossed my arms in front of me and backed up. "So that's why you kissed her? To be a *good guy*?"

"Believe it or not, a lot of women come on to me." He

pushed off the door. "Also believe it or not, I don't fuck them all, or kiss them all. She just caught me off—"

"Not all, just some." I pointed to the door. "You need to leave."

"Hell no." He took another step inside the room. "I'm not going anywhere until you listen to me. I've spent the last three days listening to *you* tell *me* how I feel, and what *I* need. Well, now it's *my* fucking turn to tell *you* how I feel."

"I'll…" I bit my tongue. "I'll call Harry on you, if you don't go."

A hollow threat if ever there was one. I wouldn't.

"Go ahead." He advanced on me, his whole body stiff and unyielding. "You want me gone, there are two ways. One: listen to me. Two: drag me out of here kicking and screaming and give the media their top story of the night. Your choice."

That's the last thing we needed. More media attention. "You wouldn't."

"Wouldn't I?" He cocked a brow. "Are you so fucking sure?"

I stared at him, biting down hard on my tongue.

He watched me with a wild look in his eyes, and he only got that look when he was determined to have his say. I'd only seen it once before, and it had been the last time we'd broken up. He'd taken on Harry to get to me. And he'd do it again.

"Fine," I bit out. "Say what you need to say."

He locked the door and tossed his keys on the table next to the door. Next went his phone. "I didn't bring that girl here to fuck her."

"You already said that."

"She was drunk, and she kissed me. I didn't kiss her back. If you'd been paying attention, you'd have seen me pull away almost immediately." He stepped even closer to me, and I forced myself to stand still. To not back down. "I didn't know I'd be here, in your hotel, till we were in the cab. And I assure you I wouldn't have brought a girl here just to hurt you like that."

LOSING *Us*

I dug my nails into my arms. Anything to stop myself from reaching out and touching him. "That's twice in a handful of days I've seen you kissing someone else, but I'm supposed to believe it wasn't by choice either time?"

He stiffened. "Yes. You're supposed to fucking trust me."

"Blindly?" I snorted. "Okay. So if you found me kissing some other guy, and I told you I hadn't kissed him—*he'd* kissed *me*—you wouldn't be upset? And then, two days later, I was kissing another guy in your hotel—but again, *I* didn't kiss *him*—you, once again, wouldn't be upset?"

He ripped off his hat and wrung it in his hands. "Of course I'd be upset, but you don't have to deal with that. Guys don't do that shit to you."

"You're right, they don't." I forced a laugh. "You want to know why?"

"Sure. Go ahead. Enlighten me."

"I don't put myself in situations where a fan thinks he is welcome to do so." I leaned in and poked a finger at his chest. "I don't flirt with guys, or make them think I like them. *You* do."

He shook his head slowly. "It's an act. It doesn't mean—"

"Oh, but it does. To them, it does." I shook my head and laughed again. "Fans are girls—just girls. And girls like you. You make them think you like them, they'll go for it. And if you think otherwise, you're a fool."

His face turned red. "I don't know how to deal with this shit, okay? I wasn't ready for this—wasn't ready for any of it. If you remember, I didn't want any of this, but you asked me to go on tour with you, and now I have it all. Everything except the one thing I wanted...*you*."

"Oh, lovely." I threw my hands up. "Now this is all my fault?"

"Yeah, maybe," he snapped back. "I didn't want to be famous or be in the public eye. I fucking told you that. But you—"

I covered my face. "I forced you to. That's what you're

going to say."

"Yes, maybe!" he shouted again. "Because look at what it fucking got me. Women throw themselves at me, and I try to be polite and have a good public image, and then I lose my girl. So, yeah, I don't fucking want this. Any of it."

"Then walk away from it all if it makes you so miserable."

"You know what?" He slammed his hat back down. "Maybe I will. Maybe I need to stop trying to be famous enough for you, or good enough for you, and I should just go back to being me."

I froze, unable to believe he'd said that. "Don't do that. Don't put that on me."

"Why not? It's true. I didn't want this," he said, flinging his arms wide to encompass the room—and *me*, I guess. "I don't need penthouses and cars and fucking fans throwing themselves at me. I just wanted you, but I tried to be that guy for you."

I shook my head. "I loved you the way you were, before the tour, and you know that. You didn't need to change for me."

"Funny, because it sure felt that way at the time." He laughed, but it was forced. "And it felt like if I wasn't famous like you, I wasn't good enough."

"No." I pushed him and he stumbled back a step. "Don't you *dare*. You know I loved you more than anything, just as you were."

"Did you?"

I dug my nails into my palms. "Yes. How could you ask me that?"

"The same way you could ask me if I wanted to be with you, and not believe me when I swore I wanted nothing more than you. And the same way you could publicly announce that we'd split, without telling me you were doing so ahead of time." He shrugged. "Love's a bitch, I guess."

"Yeah, I guess so," I managed to say.

He advanced on me. "And, yeah, those girls kissed me before I could react, and I should have set better boundaries with them. Maybe I should have seen it coming and avoided it. And maybe I'm a fucking idiot that has no idea what to do with fans, this life, or even love itself. But that doesn't mean I don't love you, or that I hate you. Not at all."

Holding a shaking hand up, I stood my ground. "Stop. Please...stop."

"But I—" He did stop, but then he crossed his arms. "I love you, damn it, and I'll always love you, but that's why this hurts so much. It's why this feels so wrong. Don't you feel that? The gut feeling that we're making the biggest mistakes of our lives by letting go of one another?"

I swallowed hard, but it was hard to get past my swollen, aching throat because I did have that feeling. It was *killing* me. "Austin..."

Something inside him seemed to deflate. It broke my heart all over again. "Fine. I give up. I didn't want to break up with you, Mac." He stepped closer, tipping my chin up. "But I need to accept it's what you want, and I accept that you're done with me. And I refuse to continue to be the bad guy here—the kind that you think likes to bring girls to your hotel to hurt you. That's not me. None of this is, and it's time to figure out who, and what, I want to be."

I nodded, holding on even tighter to my arms. I couldn't reply right now.

"How long are you going to be here in Key West?" He dropped his hold on my chin, backing up a few steps. "Because, I'm gonna be honest. Having you here hurts like hell. I need space if I'm supposed to move on."

Closing my eyes, I let out a deep breath. "I know. It hurts me, too, but the girls will be here soon. I can't leave. I promised them a fun trip."

"Far be it for me to ruin your *fun*," he said, his voice hard.

"That's not fair." I dropped my arms to my sides. "None of this is fun or fair or right. And I don't want any of this any more than you do."

"Then why did you break up with me?"

I flinched. "Because you needed it. You need to experience life without me—your new life. I'm not going to be the dead weight hanging on to your feet, refusing to let go when you try to break free."

"Who said I wanted to break free?" he asked, his voice so low I barely heard him. "Oh, that's right. *You* did."

"No, you did," I said, shaking my head and moving a step away. My back hit the wall. "Not me. I just did what you couldn't do."

"What was that?"

"I gave you an excuse to walk away." I lowered my head, not wanting to see the look in his eyes. He watched me with a mixture of anger and sadness. "And you did, didn't you? And then you kissed another girl or two. Who knows how many there were?"

He grabbed my chin and forced my head up. "It doesn't matter what I say to that, does it? Because you don't believe me."

God, I wanted to. I wanted to so badly.

"That's what I thought." He grabbed his stuff off the table and headed for the door. "I'll go now."

"Austin…" I took one step after him, and then another. "Wait."

He froze, his hand on his phone. "What?"

"I'm sorry," I whispered.

"Yeah, I am too."

And then he opened the door and left.

I stood there, staring at the door for an unknown amount of time. And I probably would have kept doing so, but the ringing of my phone snapped me out of it.

Reaching down, I saw it was a video conference call with Cassie and Quinn. I took a calming breath, swiped my hands under my eyes, and answered it. "Hey, girls. What's shakin'?"

Quinn's laugh rang through the speaker. Her eyes looked bright, so I could tell this call was about something good, and I could use something good right now, so my responding smile

LOSING *Us*

was genuine. "Two things. One, we want to be sure you're okay. The last time we spoke, you broke up with Austin," Quinn said.

I forced my smile to remain in place. "I'm hanging in. Throwing myself into work, you know? Maybe I'll get another top country hit due to my broken heart."

Cassie bit her lip. "I'm so sorry, Mac. We hate him. Like, we hate him so bad if we lay eyes on him, he's toast."

Quinn nodded. "Yeah, worse than toast. Hey, do you need us? I know we're coming out soon but hell, we'll jump on the next plane and be drinking cocktails on the beach within twenty-four hours."

Knowing they meant every word, despite the crazy lives they led, made me tear up. I sniffed and wiped my eye, refusing to cry *again*. "Well, now you're gonna make me cry and ruin my makeup. Absolutely not. I'm busy, too, and trying to clear my schedule so we can spend some quality time together. What's the second thing you called for?"

Quinn brightened. "I have good news."

I leaned in, smiling. "Good, we need it. Tell all."

"I got the full-time position at New Beginnings!"

Cassie and I both flipped out, hooting and cheering and making fools of ourselves. This was excellent news. It deserved a standing ovation. "I can't wait to celebrate!" I shouted out. "Congratulations, darling. You so deserve it."

"I never doubted you," Cassie said, her own smile huge. "Do you start after graduation?"

"Yes, I already put in for vacation for spring break, so that's still clear."

"I bet James is just as excited," Cassie mentioned.

"I'm waiting to tell him. Figured I'd call my girls first."

"You better!" I warned. "Forget that 'bros before hoes' crap. It's BFFs before boyfriends!"

We all laughed, chattered a bit, and finally ended the call.

And the smile stayed, even after, despite my own heartache.

CHAPTER
Fourteen

Austin

I steepled my fingers under my chin and locked eyes on my agent. His brown hair was frazzled. Almost as frazzled as he was. He paced back and forth, his belly proceeding him by at least six inches with each step. Ever since I'd fought with Mac last night, I'd been so sure that I knew what I needed. What I wanted.

Who I wanted to be.

"You can't do this," said my agent, Lou, pacing back and forth in front of me. "It's career suicide."

"Does it really matter in the long run?" I asked.

After all, I'd never wanted to be famous.

Not since I'd come back from California and created a life for Rachel and me. I was her brother, yes, but more importantly, I was the father she'd never had. How many times during the past six months had I missed something in her life?

LOSING Us

Right now, she was off checking out a college with her best friend's family—instead of with me.

My priorities had shifted ever since I'd met and fallen in love with Mac. It was time to go back to the way things were. Yes, we'd been tight on money back then, and we'd been struggling to make ends meet. Yes, we'd had more struggles than that, and they'd been real.

But I'd been *there*.

And she's known she could count on me. Could she still?

"Of course it does," he snapped, glaring at me. "This is your livelihood."

I dropped my hands to my lap. "I don't care. I don't want it."

"This is a huge deal, with a huge advance. I don't think you realize the amount of money we're talking about." He stopped in front of me, his ruddy cheeks redder than usual. "We're talking videos. Tours. A full support PR team. A—"

"Know what I hear in all that?" I stood up. "Me, being away. Me, fighting to balance family and my career, and failing. I've already been down this road."

"But now you have it all figured out, right?"

"Yeah, I do. And something's gotta give." I headed for the door, but stopped and pointed at the paparazzi waiting for me. "It's this life. I don't need or want it. I don't want the attention or the hype. I'm not even with Mackenzie anymore. Soon, if I stop giving them music, they'll forget all about me."

"That's what I'm scared of."

"But it's what I want." I shook my head. "I didn't want this. I got caught up in the whole thing, and I was trying to be someone..."

"You know what I think? *I* think you're making this decision because of a girl," my agent said. "I know you're upset about Mackenzie, but now is not the time to make these decisions."

"Oh, I disagree. I think it's the perfect fucking time."

"Take some time and think about it for a few days before

we make any rash decisions. Maybe…" He snapped his fingers. "I've got it. Take a break from touring until your sister graduates, but release some songs here and there on a YouTube channel. That's all the rage now."

"You don't get it. I don't want to be all the rage. I want to sing in my bar, and I want to be home. I want to be there for Rachel." I slashed a hand through the air. "That's it. I haven't signed anything yet, so I can back out if I want."

He sputtered. "Take a few days and think before you act. Talk to Rachel and maybe your accountant or something. At least give me that."

"Fine," I gritted out. "But don't expect me to change my mind."

"And if you don't, what am I supposed to tell them?"

"I don't give a damn what you tell them," I said, opening the door. "As long as you get the job done, if it comes to that."

As I walked outside, the paps scurried like rats, taking pictures of me as quickly as they could. "How did it go? When can we expect your album to hit the shelves?"

I ducked my head and kept walking, ignoring them. They'd all be gone soon enough. And no one would give a damn what Austin Murphy, bartender and part-time singer, did with his fucking life. I. Couldn't. Wait.

Sliding into the driver's seat of my Jetta, I drove home, my music blaring the whole time. It was the first time I'd felt so free—so light—in months. No looming deadlines hanging over my head. No worries. I was free to be me, and not give a damn what I said or did. I didn't have Mac anymore. I didn't have my career.

And I'd be fine.

Why, then, didn't I feel fine?

When I pulled up to my driveway, it was just in time to see Kaitlyn's parents' van pull away from the curb. That meant Rachel was home.

Good. We'd get pizza, catch up on *The Walking Dead*, and she could tell me all about her weekend. And I'd get to tell her that come hell or high water...

Next time, I'd be there with her.

I hopped out of the car and walked up the driveway, my steps light. As I opened the door, I called out, "Honey, I'm home."

"In here!" she yelled from the kitchen. I followed it and entered the kitchen. She scrounged around in the fridge, shoving stuff to the side, her long brown hair hiding her face from me. "Do we have any OJ?"

"No," I walked into the room and leaned against the entry, crossing my arms and my ankles. "How did it go?"

"It looked nice enough, I guess," she answered dismissively, tapping her fingers on the handle of the fridge before closing it and facing me with eyes that were identical to mine. "How are you doing?"

"Fine," I said. "I'm fine."

"What happened?" she asked, nibbling on her lower lip. "I mean, I've read the stories online and all, but I'd rather have the real one from you."

"What did you read?"

"You broke her heart. Cheated on her." She pinched her lips together. "And then there's another going around that we were too much for her. The poor tortured boy and his little sister weren't famous enough for America's Sweetheart, or something like that."

"No. That's not true." I walked up to her and rested a hand on her shoulder, squeezing slightly. "We just didn't work out. There were things...personal things...but we fought. She thought I didn't want to be with her, so she...freed me. Her words, not mine."

She cocked her head to the side. She looked so much like our mother when she did that. It almost hurt to look at her. She had Dad's eyes, like me, but they weren't cold like his...or mine. "But did you want to be free?"

"Absolutely not." I hesitated, dropping my hold on her. "But I did realize I got swept up in the whole lifestyle she has.

The fame, the shows, the tour."

"What's so wrong with that?"

"I miss things. I miss you, and important things like your college tours." I rubbed my temples and sighed. "I'm never around anymore, Rach. This isn't what I wanted. I came home to take care of you, and I will. I'm done chasing dreams and fame. Done with the press and the media and the rumors. I just want to go back to being normal."

"But you're not normal." She grabbed my hand and dragged me to the window, pulling the curtains back a little bit. Out front, two reporters camped out, waiting for a shot of me. "You never will be normal. Those guys are out there because you're special, and you can't give that up. Not because you feel guilty for missing a stupid college tour."

"But I'm supposed to be there," I argued. "I'm your guardian."

"Yeah, but you were busy making money to send me to that college, or whatever college I end up picking," she said, smiling gently. She might only be seventeen, but she was acting like such an adult right now. More so than I was. I was a fucking mess right now. I'd never been more proud of her. "Don't give up your dreams for me, or because you're upset over Mac."

"You sound like my agent," I muttered.

"That's because he's right. And so am I." She let the curtain fall back into place. "And, now, for my lecture about her…"

"Don't," I said, my voice hard. "It's over. She doesn't want to be with me anymore. She made that quite clear, numerous times."

She rolled her eyes. "No offense, but you're a guy, so I don't trust your instinct. She said she set you free, but *why*? Was it because she didn't love you anymore, or was it *for you*? Did she say?"

"She said she did what I couldn't do. She gave me an excuse to walk away, and be free to see other women. She thought I wanted that."

Biting down on her lip, she shook her head. "You have to

LOSING *Us*

go to her and fix it. She didn't break up with you for her, she did it for *you*. She still loves you."

"Love isn't always enough. She said so."

"Then give her more. Show her how much you love her. Prove her wrong. Show her you want to be with her and not some random girl." She crossed her arms. "What have you done to show her you feel that way since she broke up with you?"

My cheeks heated. "Uh…" *Kissed another girl in her lobby.* "I…"

"Yeah, that's what I thought."

I sat down on the couch. "I don't know what to do," I admitted, running my hands through my hair. "I don't know anything about love, really."

"Sure you do. You've been loving me for years."

"That's different." I glanced up at her, resting my forearms on my knees and leaning my weight on them. "You're my sister."

"But it's not. Not really." She sat beside me. "If she's upset, she needs you to show you care about her. Simple, really."

"If you say so. I tried to tell her I didn't want to be free or anything. She didn't believe me."

"Show, don't tell."

I cocked a brow. "Meaning?"

"Woo her. Show her how much she means to you."

"Shouldn't she know?" I asked, scratching my head. "I told her I still love her, and I used to tell her all the time. Those words don't come lightly from me. If I say I love her, I mean it. I'll love her forever, whether or not she's with me. I'll love her no matter what she says, does, or thinks. I'll love her no matter what happens. Zombies, plague, war. She'll always come first with me. Always. She should *know* that."

She squeezed my knee. "Tell her again, but use those words. Exactly. And maybe add in a few more pretty ones. She needs to hear that."

"But—"

"Just try it for me, okay?" She stood up and tugged me to my feet. "Go to her now. Make this right. Tell her you love her, and more importantly? Show her."

I stood shakily, my heart thudding hard. "About this whole singing thing…I do want to take a step back. I don't want to go on tour. I don't want to be gone all the time."

"Then don't. But you can't just stop."

"I don't know…"

"I do. You might not be so sure, but you want this. You do." She smiled. "You're just too busy worrying about me, but I like that you're doing what you love. I think it's awesome. I hope to one day love my job as much as you love yours."

"I'm sure you will." I hugged her and kissed the top of her head. "You'll be an awesome doctor. Love you, kid."

"I love you too." She pushed my chest lightly. "Now go say that to Mac, and put this modern family of ours back together."

"But you just got home. I want to spend time with you," I protested.

"I'm going to eat, shower, and then study." She pushed me again. "You're not missing anything. Now *go*."

I walked out the door on autopilot, my keys in my hand and my hat on my head. As I walked toward my car, cameramen snapped pics. I ignored them. The whole way to the hotel, I ran over our conversation for the millionth time.

Keeping Rachel's words in mind about showing instead of telling, I stopped at the store and got Mac pink tulips. They were her favorite flowers. I'd give them to her, tell her all the things I'd said to Rachel, and then I'd try my best to show her how much I meant them all. I had no idea what that meant, but I'd figure it out…or I'd be fucked.

I couldn't lose her for good. I *had* to fix this before it was too late.

Before she moved on.

As I walked into the lobby, I stuck my free hand in my pocket and walked over to Harry, smiling when he glared at my flowers and me. "Hey, buddy. Long time, no see. How's the wife? And the kids?"

His chest puffed. "Get out."

"I can't." I rested the flowers against my chest. "I need to talk to her."

"Get out," he repeated. "She cried for an hour last night after you left. I'm not letting her suffer through that again."

"I don't want to make her cry," I said, my heart wrenching at the idea that I'd done so last night. Again. "I want to make her smile, laugh, and be happy."

Harry crossed his arms. "Then leave her alone. You're broken up, right?"

"Maybe, but I don't want to be. She thinks I do, but she's wrong. She's very wrong." I rocked back on my heels and lowered the flowers to hip level. A single pink petal hit the floor. "I need to go up unannounced, make my big speech, and beg her to take me back. I love her, man. Give me a shot to prove it to her."

"So bringing a girl here last night was a way to show her that?"

"No." I squared my jaw, getting an annoying sense of *deja vu* from this whole thing. I'd had to beg to be let through the last time we'd broken up. "That was all a big misunderstanding. Do you think I'd be here, arguing with you, holding flowers in my hand, if I didn't love her? Just let me through, man. C'mon."

"Last time I let you up, you made it good for a little while, but then ruined it again. Why should I let you up now?" he asked, staring at me with murder in his eyes.

"Because I love her, and so do you."

Harry stared at me without speaking, his brown eyes darker than ever before. "You don't want to go up there right now, man. Go home."

"No." I stared right back at him, fully prepared to do battle all night if that's what it took to get past him. "*Please.*"

The elevator doors opened, and Mac stepped out, a tall guy next to her. I'd never met him, but I recognized him right away. He was a fellow country singer, one Mac had often spoken of fondly. His brown eyes were on her, and she laughed at something he said. For all intents and purposes, she looked good.

Happy, even.

Damn her. And damn me too.

"I don't know yet, but we'll see after dinner," she said, smiling up at him. "I might be persuaded."

"I have very strong powers of persuasion," the blond guy said, grinning. He was only a year or so older than Mac, if I recalled correctly, and he'd recently broken up with a fiancée. A normal girl, not a star. The very thing I'd been trying to avoid. "You'll see."

She laughed and stepped out of the elevator. "I'm sure I'll—"

One foot in the air, she froze and stared at me, her green eyes wide. Her curly hair fell around her face in gentle waves, and I noticed immediately that she'd dyed it back to her original color. Light blonde. She looked so young and free and pretty…it hurt. I felt like shit, and she was out laughing with other guys, wearing a pretty pink dress, and going on a date.

Rachel had been wrong.

"Harry, what's going on?" she asked, her hands worrying her small clutch purse. Her gaze fell to the stupid flowers I'd brought before slowly raising back to my face. "Why are you two standing off against one another with…?"

Fucking flowers. Just say it.

The country dude stepped beside her and placed a hand on the small of her back. "What's wrong? What's going on?"

"I am," I said, my voice uneven. "I'm sorry to interrupt. I didn't know you had…company tonight. I'll, uh, go."

The guy whose name escaped me stepped forward, a friendly smile on his face. "Hey, you're Austin Murphy, right?"

I shook his hand even though I'd rather punch him right on his fucking nose. His perfect, as yet unbroken, nose. Mine had been broken twice before I turned fifteen. Both times by my asshole dad. I tucked the flowers behind my back, even

LOSING Us

though he'd already seen them. "Yeah. And you are…?"

"Luke Granger." He dropped my hand and returned his to the small of Mac's back. "Nice to meet you, man. I've heard a lot about you."

I flicked my glance over to Mac, who watched me intently, her face pale and gaunt. Her attention was locked on the hand behind my back. "Hopefully not all bad," I managed to say, despite my aching head and heart.

Luke laughed. "Of course not."

We all fell silent awkwardly, just kind of staring at one another, and then I realized why. Because these two were going on a date, and her ex was gaping at them.

Fucking idiot.

I stepped back. "Well, I'll—"

"Austin—" Mac said at the same time. "What?"

"No, you go first," I said, forcing a smile.

Mac wrung her purse in front of her. "I…uh…" She glanced at Luke. "I was just going to say we have to go. We have reservations at six."

"Right. Of course." I shoved my free hand back into my jeans and stepped back, swallowing hard. I kept the flowers hidden behind my back. "Have a lovely dinner. You look very beautiful in that dress, Mac."

"Thanks," Mac said, her green eyes locked on me so hard I could feel them boring through my head. It was as if she could see right through me, and knew seeing her with another guy was killing me. She was right. It hurt more than any beating I could have gotten from my father. "This isn't…we're not…I…"

I waited, but she didn't finish. "Please. Don't let me stop you two. I was just chatting with Harry here. Catching up, ya know?"

"You weren't here to see me?" she asked.

"What do you think?" I asked, my grip tightening on the stems. "Anyway… Have a nice night."

She hesitated but nodded once and walked out the door with Luke. As I watched, flashes went off, and they posed for the cameras like good little stars.

Something I'd never be.

My grip on the flowers tightened even more, and I could feel the jagged edges of the one rose I'd hidden inside the bouquet dig into my hand. It had been my way of saying she was a rose among tulips. One of a kind. Special.

Something else I'd never be.

Harry cleared his throat. "Look, man…"

"Yeah. I know. Get out." I glanced over at him, forcing my eyes off the gorgeous, wholesome, clean-cut pair as they slid into a waiting town car, all smiles and happiness. "I just need a minute. You can go on. They're waiting for you."

"I'm sorry you had to see that," Harry said. "But the way you handled it showed me something your words didn't."

I didn't look at him because I couldn't stop staring at the place where Mac had left with Luke, perfect and together. They made sense. Sense that we never would. Everything I'd ever wanted had walked out that door, and there had been nothing I could do to stop it. "What's that?"

"You really do love her."

I finally tore my eyes off the door, fighting every urge I had inside me to run outside, chase the car down, and drag her out and into my arms. "Because I let her go?"

"Because you cared enough not to make a scene." Harry uncrossed his arms. "If you'd been immature and made a few jabs at her, I'd have kicked your ass."

"She…I love her. She's my life. And I…" I shook my head and backed up. "I can't do this. I can't."

Pivoting on my heel, I headed for the doors on the other side of the lobby, tossing the flowers into the trash can as I went. I loved her, and she'd moved on. It was over.

I'd already lost.

CHAPTER Fifteen

Mackenzie

Later that night, I walked out of the bathroom in my hotel, toweling my face dry. I'd taken a long, hot shower, and then a long, hot bath. Once I'd run out of hot water, I'd finally come out, but I still hadn't felt clean. Going on that "date" with Luke, had been harder than I'd have thought it would ever be. And it hadn't even been a *real* date. Just a way to pull attention off the fact that both of us had been seen broken hearted every night on the TV since our breakups.

A stupid publicity thing my PR team made me do.

I'd hated every second of it. We'd spent the whole night talking about how much we missed our exes and how miserable we both were before turning the talk toward work. Tour schedules, recording sessions, and sales. Then we'd talked about a possible duet, which he'd been trying to convince me of when we'd stepped off the elevator...and found Austin in the lobby. Holding *flowers*.

When I'd gotten back, he'd been gone, and so had the flowers. A knock sounded on the door, and my heart picked up speed. Smoothing my wet hair over my head, I opened the door with a trembling hand. When I saw it was Harry and not Austin, my heart sank a little bit more. I forced a smile and asked, "Hey. What's up?"

"I pulled these out of the trash." Harry brandished the flowers Austin had brought from behind his back, his brown eyes shining more than his bald brown head. "Thought you might want them."

I reached out and took the vase of flowers. He'd removed them from the packaging and put them in water. As I pulled them to my nose, I blinked down at the one rose in the middle. It stood out like a sore thumb. "Uh…there's a rose in here."

"Yeah." Harry shrugged and held out a small card. "I don't know why, but it was in the bouquet. You'd have to ask him. He had a note in it too."

I nodded, took the note, and Harry walked off. I watched him go, then shut the door. Leaning against it, I closed my eyes and held the vase to my chest, breathing fast. After setting the flowers on the floor, I opened the card.

I might not be good at love, and my love might not be enough for us to be happy, but you have it and always will. I will never give up on you…on us. Not in a million years. If you're wondering why I put a rose in here, that's you. You're one of a kind. I guess it's also our love. Hell, us. Standing out in a crowd of faces. We can make it through this, if you want to. If you want me. I love you, Mac.

I walked over to the table by the door, set the flowers down, and picked up my phone. The note, I held clutched to my chest. It only took me three seconds before I remembered he'd changed his number…and hadn't given me the new one. "Crap."

Setting the phone back down, I leaned on the table, gripping the edge and staring at myself in the mirror. Green

LOSING *Us*

eyes reflected back at me, watching me with judgment. So much freaking judgment.

"Your move, Mac," I said, staring back at myself.

Picking the phone back up, I went on Twitter and typed in Austin's name. His feed popped up, and I swallowed hard and scanned his tweets during the past twenty-four hours. He'd tweeted something about a football game the other day, but besides that, the last thing he'd tweeted was he couldn't wait to see me in Nashville.

It had gotten more than two thousand favorites and four thousand retweets.

Swallowing hard, I opened a direct message and typed: *I got the flowers*. As I waited to see if he'd reply, I sat down on the couch, my eyes locked on the bouquet. When he didn't reply, I typed, *I like the rose*.

Still nothing.

He obviously wasn't on his phone right now, so I could either sit back, waiting for him to see it at some point, or I could take the excuse I had to hunt him down. Chances were, he'd either be at home or Captain Crow's. Standing up, I threw on a gray dress, a pair of boots, and a cowboy hat. There really wasn't anything to debate here. After reading that note, I *had* to see him. Had to know why he'd come by earlier…

And why he'd brought me flowers.

As I entered the lobby, Harry looked up and grinned. "Going somewhere?"

"Yeah. You know exactly where I'm going."

He followed me. "I'll drive with you to his house."

As we walked to the car, no one snapped pictures. It was a miracle they were all busy elsewhere. Maybe some other celebrity was making a fool of themselves, therefore creating a bigger story than me. We made it to Austin's house in a matter of minutes, and I let out a sigh of relief when I saw his Jetta in the driveway.

He was home. Rachel's lights were out in her room, and so were Austin's, but the TV was on downstairs, judging from the flickering lights.

I sat in the car for a second, not moving, nervous as heck.

"You got this." Harry smiled and patted me on the back. "If you want me to help or need anything, call."

"I will. Go back to the hotel," I said, my eyes locked on that flickering light downstairs. "I'll call for the driver when I'm ready to be picked up. Get some sleep."

"Only if you're staying here." He shifted his weight and rested a hand against the glass window. "No wondering off, or going out without me."

"I promise." Leaning close, I kissed his cheek. "You take good care of me. Thank you for that."

"Then listen to me. That boy loves you." He leaned back and pointed to the house. "He might not be the best at showing it, but I saw him after you came down with Luke today, and I saw him before that too. He was going to fight for you."

"He doesn't have to fight." I opened the door and stepped out. Once I stood, I leaned in, resting my hands on the car. "He just has to love me and want me."

"Well, then, good luck."

I nodded and closed the door, smoothing the dress I'd thrown on over my unsteady legs. As I walked up the driveway, I glanced over my shoulder at Harry, who gave me a thumbs up. I didn't know exactly what I was going to say, or what would happen, but he'd come to me tonight. It was my turn to go to him.

He'd been right, in a way, last night. I'd decided how he felt and just...reacted. Without believing him when he said he hadn't meant those things. Without believing him when he said he loved me and didn't want to be free. I hadn't listened.

Now, I was ready. I was ready to listen.

I missed him, and if I was right...he missed me.

When I reached the porch, I took a calming breath, tugged my hat lower, lifted my hand, and knocked three times. I could hear something on the TV through the door, and I thought I heard my name, but I could have been wrong.

LOSING *Us*

A bang, followed by a curse, and then the door swung open. Austin peeked through the crack, blinked at me, glanced over his shoulder, and then blinked at me again. "Am I asleep?"

"No. You're awake." I swallowed hard and grabbed the hem of my dress, squeezing it in my hands. "Can I please come in?"

He leaned his head on the door and sighed. It took me all of a second to notice two things. One: he was shirtless, which showed off his abs and all that black ink perfectly to my starved eyes. And two: he had a drink in his hand.

And was maybe already drunk.

"Did you have a nice date?" he asked, his blue eyes dark and stormy. "Come to tell me all about it, or what?"

I shook my head once. "Are you going to let me in?"

"Depends. Did you kiss him?"

"No." I crossed my arms. "Not even close. You kiss anyone else since the girl in my lobby?"

"Nope." He stepped back, opening the door and motioning me inside with the hand that held a half-full glass of whiskey. "Not even close."

"Is Rachel home?" I asked, surveying the living room. I'd been right, he'd been watching TV, and they were talking about Luke and me. "Or is she still away?"

"She came home earlier," he said, walking past me and then settling in his chair. He slung an arm over the side of the chair, his glass perched at his fingertips. He looked seconds from dropping it. Totally relaxed and okay with all this, when I was a nervous wreck. "She's asleep, though, so if you came to see her, you're too late."

"I came to see you," I said, sitting down across from him. "How drunk are you?"

He lifted a shoulder. "Not drunk enough to stop feeling the pain, but drunk enough to dull it the tiniest of tiny bits."

The half-empty bottle of whiskey sat in front of him on the coffee table, and I picked it up. "Well, then...bottoms up."

Saluting him, I tipped my head back and swallowed a big gulp. It tasted like acid, but I didn't care. Swiping my forearm across my mouth, I leaned back and studied him. He watched me through narrowed eyes, his chest rising and falling with each breath.

"You drink whiskey now?"

I shrugged. "I do tonight, yeah."

"Why tonight?" he asked, those bright blue eyes of his locked on me.

Smirking, I used his most common response back on him. "Why do you think I'm drinking whiskey tonight?"

The commercial break ended behind me, and the reporter continued. "*Has Mackenzie Forbes moved on from bad boy Austin Murphy? Our sources say yes! She was spotted today in Miami with country's golden boy Luke Granger, getting cozy over dinner. Could you think of a better match than those two? We can't. Sources say they were snuggling, laughing, and even shared dessert. Looks like America's Sweetheart has moved on to greener—*"

The TV shut off. Austin tossed the remote aside and finished his drink. "Assholes. All of them."

"I got your flowers."

He flexed his jaw. "How? I threw them out."

"Harry got them out of the can."

"Oh." He shifted his weight in his chair. "You didn't throw them away again?"

"No." I hesitated. "They're pretty."

"Not as pretty as you." He winced. "Fuck, that was corny as hell. Ignore that."

"It wasn't corny. It was sweet." I offered the bottle to him, and he held his glass out. I poured him two fingers and lifted the bottle back to my lips. "Don't mind if I do."

He watched me as I took another gulp. "What are you doing?"

"Drinking whiskey." I set the bottle down. "What's it look like I'm doing?"

He sat forward, resting his weight on his elbows and knees. "You know what I mean. Why are you here, drinking with me?"

"To see why you came to my hotel. And to talk about the flowers...and the note. The things you said in that note..." I picked up the bottle and took another gulp. He snatched it away the second I lowered it. "Hey. Give that back."

"You're going to make yourself sick," he said, his voice hard.

"I don't want to be sick. I just want to be drunk. To loosen up a bit. I'm so tired of being the one who worries all the time." I stood up and stumbled a bit to the side. "Oops. Might already be a little drunk."

He steadied me, his mouth pressed into a tight line. "What do you mean about being the one who worries all the time?"

"That's why I broke up with you. I was worried you weren't happy, and to be honest? You didn't give me a reason to think I was wrong...until tonight." I walked over to the picture of him and Rachel. She looked about two years younger, and he looked harder than he was now. Colder. More cynical. It hurt my heart. I could feel his eyes on me, so I tried to think of something to say. "You know, I don't even have your phone number anymore. That kind of sucks."

He stood, too, and came up behind me. "Why? Do you want it?"

I touched the picture, tracing the hard edge of his jaw. "How old were you here? You look so...different. Harder."

"Twenty-two. It was the day the courts granted me guardianship over Rachel, after Dad tried to kill her, and I almost killed him." He set his glass down on the table. "But you already knew that, didn't you?"

I licked my lips. "Yeah..."

"And since you asked earlier, I came to your hotel because I wanted to see you." He shifted on his feet. "To talk to you."

"What did you want to say?" I licked my lips and lifted my face to his. "Why did you bring me those flowers?"

His jaw flexed. "Why do you think I'd bring you flowers?"

There it was again. That stupid question that wasn't really

a question. "Austin…"

"Fine." He pinched the bridge of his nose. I'd always liked his nose. It had been broken a few times, but that showed me how strong he was. What he'd been through, and what he'd accomplished. "I came because I'm not okay. I'm not okay at all, but it seems like you are. And that fucking hurts."

I shook my head. "I'm not okay, either."

"And I came because Rachel told me I had to show you how much I love you, instead of just saying it all the time." He locked eyes with me, the bright blue color seeming almost translucent. "I miss you. I love you, and I can't live without you. It's not just that I don't want to. I don't. But I also *can't*, Mac. I can't do it."

Swallowing back tears, I stepped closer. "I don't, and can't, either."

He continued on as if he didn't hear me. "And every second I spend apart from you kills me a little bit more. When I saw you with that guy—that guy who's a million times better for you than I will ever be—it hurt so much I'd wished, for just a second, that I'd never met you. Never fallen in love with you and lost you. It would hurt less."

"No. Austin…"

He cupped my cheek, his touch tender and gentle, despite the rawness of his voice. The hurt and anger that lied beneath his words. "But then I took it all back immediately, because knowing you—*loving* you—has been a privilege. I'm just sad it's one I don't get to keep."

My heart beat loudly in my head, drowning out everything but him. This moment. "That's what you wanted to say?"

"Yes. And that…" He lifted his head and locked eyes with me, the intensity of his stare sucking me in until I drowned in their blue depths. "I don't want to be free. I want to be attached to you—hook, line and sinker. I don't want to screw other women. I want to love you. I love you so damn much, and until you…I didn't even know what that kind of love was, or what it felt like. I didn't know any of it, but now that I do, I can't stand it anymore."

I blinked at him. "What do you mean?"

"Love fucking hurts. And it sucks. You said love isn't always enough." He stepped back and dragged his hands down his face. "What does that even mean? What more do you want from me, if my love isn't enough? I swear that I'll give it to you, whatever it is. I'll get the fucking moon out of the sky if that's what it takes to get you back. To prove to you that I can be enough. I'll do it."

I took a step toward him but made myself stop. If I touched him, we'd stop talking. And we needed to talk. My heart wrenched at the pain in his voice, in every move he made. "All I've ever wanted is for you to be happy. Whatever makes you happy, you should have it. What makes you happy, Austin?"

He cupped my face with both of his hands, his fingers trembling as he looked down at me with so much love and pain in his eyes. It echoed my own. "*You.*"

"Austin…" I closed my eyes. "If that's what you want…"

"And I'm sorry that I said those things about not liking being saddled down to one woman, and even sorrier that I gave you a reason to think I meant them when I didn't." He dropped his forehead to mine and let out a shaky breath. "And I'm even more sorry that I hurt you so many times, in so many ways, but I have no fucking clue what the hell I'm doing here. None."

I laughed lightly, tears blurring my vision. "Yeah, me neither."

"All I know is I love you with everything I have inside of me, and then some more. I know I don't want to live a life where you're not in it. And I know I don't deserve you. Not in a million years." He lowered his face to mine, a breath away from kissing me. "But I also know I'll never stop trying to. If you let me, I'll love you forever and ever, and nothing will make me stop. Nothing in this world, the next, or the last. You will be forever tattooed on my heart, and the letters will never fade."

"I love you too. So much." I gripped his biceps, digging my fingers in. If I had it my way, I'd never let go of him again. "So freaking much. And you've always been enough."

His fingers tightened on my face. "Are you saying what I think you're saying?"

"I'm saying yes." I tilted my face up, my lips touching his as I said, "Kiss me. Love me. Keep me. Hold me tight, and don't ever let me go."

He made a broken sound and kissed me, his lips crashing over mine. The second our mouths met, everything faded away. All the worry, the doubt, the pain.

It was all healed, with one magical kiss.

CHAPTER Sixteen

Austin

I tightened my grip and entwined my tongue with hers, backing her against the wall with a predatory growl. After she'd left with that Luke kid, I'd been prepared to let her go gracefully. Lose with my head held high, in public at least. Been prepared to admit she was better off without me darkening her bright life, continually making her life stormy and tumultuous.

But then she'd come into my house and asked me what I wanted. And I wanted her, damn it. All of her. Forever. This time, I wouldn't let her go.

This time, I wouldn't lose her.

Some small voice in the back of my head whispered that she was only kissing me and saying these things because she'd downed a shitload of whiskey, but I told it to shut the hell up. She said she loved me, and I loved her, and we would be okay.

We *had* to be okay.

But still, I broke off the kiss and rested my forehead on hers. "Are you sure? Are you…are you all in?"

"I'm all in," she breathed, burying her hands in my hair and tugging on it. "I love you, and you're enough. You were always enough. Don't ever doubt that. Whether you're a singer, a bartender, the President of the United States, or a stay-at-home dad—you're enough for me. Always have been."

My heart cracked, broke apart, and melted. I swung her in my arms, letting that damn hat of hers hit the floor. "I love you. I missed you. I need you. I love you," I whispered, kissing her repeatedly, over and over again, as I carried her into my bedroom.

As soon as I locked the door behind us, I set her on her feet and ravaged her mouth, giving no quarter as I backed her toward the bed, pulling her dress up slowly, inch by inch. When I bared her ass, I cupped her and hauled her against my body. She gripped my belt, undoing it frantically as I smacked her ass gently.

Whimpering, she fell back on the bed, my belt still in her grip, so she dragged me with her. I landed exactly where I wanted to be—in between her legs.

She rolled her hips against me, moaning and running her fingers up my bare back. I broke off the kiss and tugged her dress over her head.

Once she lay beneath me in a sheer bra and skimpy matching panties, I ran my thumb over her cheekbones, taking in every detail of her face. "I want to marry you someday, Mac. I just want you to know that."

Her eyes widened, and she licked those lips of hers I loved so much. "Is that a proposal?"

"Yes and no." I kissed her gently. "I'll do it right, and be romantic and all that shit, but for now, know this one thing: I want you to be my wife. My family. My life."

"Yes," she breathed, smiling up at me with tears in her eyes.

"I didn't ask yet…" I teased, kissing her on the tip of the

nose. "I know I'm a mess, and I don't know how to show my feelings all that great, and odds are I'll fuck up again. But if I do, and I hurt you, please don't ever doubt my love. You never know what life will throw at you, but you can count on one thing: I'll never stop loving you. Ever."

"I'll never stop loving you, either." She rested her hand on my heart, smiling. "With all my heart. Forever and always. Don't *you* ever doubt that."

I shook my head, pressing our foreheads together. "I won't. Not ever again. And when we fight...which we're going to do...let's take time to work it through before we call it quits."

She nodded. "Yes. So much yes. I'm sorry I jumped the gun."

"We're both sorry, but we made it through our first big fight." I grinned down at her, unable to believe she was here, with me, in my arms. And we were talking about forever again. For-fucking-ever. "That's some kind of milestone, right?"

"I think so."

I saw her phone on the table, grabbed it, and unlocked it. "I have an idea."

"What?" she asked. As I opened the camera, she scrunched her face up. "Is this *really* the best selfie time?"

"Yep." I flicked it to video and hit record. The second it started, I smiled. "Hey, sweetheart, it's me. I wanted to make you this little video so that next time we get in a fight, or miss each other, we can remember this moment. See that woman under me?" I panned the camera to her, and she laughed. "That's you. I love you very much, and I never, ever want another woman to be under me like this. Like we are."

"Austin..." She looked up at me, instead of the camera, and the love I saw shining in her eyes made my heart skip a beat. The idea that a girl like her could look at me like that, and love me so much, was almost terrifying. "I love you so much. I'll never want to be with another man like I'm with you, and I'll never stop being yours. And I want to marry you someday. Any day. Anywhere. Any time."

My fingers tightened on the phone, and I forced a smile. "See, future Mac and Austin? We love each other, and that will never, ever change. I'm going to make love to you now, so I'm gonna shut this off. But don't be idiots next time. Talk before acting."

Shutting off the camera, I tossed the phone to the side. Slipping my hand between her legs, I rubbed my thumb against her clit. She was so wet. So ready for me. And, damn it, I was ready for her.

"Oh my God," she breathed.

Nibbling on her ear, I bit down a little harder. She moaned and arched her neck for me. "Every time we fight, we'll watch that video. Deal?"

She nodded frantically. "Deal."

"Good."

Without another word, I kissed her, my fingers moving over her in hard sweeps. I dropped kisses down her body as I went. One on her throat. Another on the gentle curve of her breast. As I kissed her all over, as I'd been dying to do for what felt like my whole fucking life, I undid her bra and tossed it aside.

Her dusky nipples were hard and begging for my touch, so I closed my mouth around one, sucking it in hard. She arched her back and tossed her head back and forth, moaning out my name. I'd never get sick of hearing my name on her lips, all needy and desperate and *mine*.

Releasing her nipple, I moved even farther down her body, nipping the skin right above her hipbone as I went. She buried her hands in my hair and opened her legs for me. Grabbing hold of the skimpy underwear, I ripped them off her and closed my mouth over her clit, moaning at how good she tasted.

"Oh my God," she breathed, her lids falling down. "*Yes.*"

I slid my hands under her ass, hauling her even tighter against my mouth. She tugged on my hair, desperation coming off her in ripples. A desperation that grew even stronger when

LOSING Us

I slapped the side of her ass gently. Her whole body tensed, and she sagged against my hold, a small moan escaping her as she came against my mouth. As I let her fall to the mattress, I positioned myself between her legs and kissed her. I still had my pants on, so I hopped off the bed and took them off. She watched me, her green eyes glowing with pleasure and love. So much fucking love.

She stretched like a cat, her blonde hair splayed across my pillow. I froze, my hands on my belt, and just took it in. All of it. Her. Me. The way she made me feel.

And I never wanted to leave this moment.

She leaned up on an elbow and watched me, her red lips pursed prettily. "You okay?"

"Okay?" I undid my pants and let them hit the floor. Next went my boxers, and I got in the bed with her, slipping between her legs where I belonged. Grabbing her leg, I hauled it up, and she wrapped it around my body securely. "I'm fucking fabulous."

Without another word, I drove inside her, kissing her as I entered her fully. She wrapped her other leg around me, locking her ankles. I pulled out, my tongue withdrawing from her mouth as I did so. As I thrust back inside, I bit down on her lip gently. Her nails dug into my back and then...

I fucking lost it.

Groaning, I moved hard and fast, needing to feel her convulse around me again. Needing to make her come again. Needing her.

She cried out and moved beneath me restlessly, her pussy getting tighter on my cock with each stroke I made. My balls tightened and tingled, and I knew I'd be there soon. I'd be in heaven, wrapped in my Mac's arms. "I love you," I whispered against her lips, lowering my hand between us to press against her. "I love you so fucking much."

"I love you...oh my God," she cried out.

Her walls tightened around me, and I groaned, pumping my hips harder and faster until I came so explosively I saw fireworks in front of my eyes. Fucking *fireworks*.

Collapsing on the bed next to her, I pulled her into my arms and closed my eyes. She wrapped herself around me, bare skin pressed to bare skin. Roughness to porcelain. So different, and yet so fucking perfect at the same time. I kissed the top of her head and tugged on a long curl. "Can you stay here with me tomorrow?"

She yawned. "The girls are coming in, and we have plans. But I'm all yours tomorrow night."

I played with a piece of her hair. "So…is it safe to say we're together again?"

"Yes." She brushed my hair back off my head. "I think it's very safe to say."

"When should we make it public?" I asked, yawning. "And how?"

"We'll think of something, I'm sure." She nuzzled her nose against my chest. "Something romantic and shit."

I snorted. "Using my words back on me again?"

"Totally."

"Forever?" I asked.

"And always," she answered, yawning at the end. "Are you going to keep recording, or are you taking a step back?"

I let out a soft breath. "I am taking a step back, but not stopping entirely. I just need to enjoy this last year with Rachel before she goes to college. You know?"

"Yeah, I do. You're such a good dad."

I smiled, because she'd called me a dad, not a brother. And that's what I was to Rachel. I needed to be a good one. One who set a good example of chasing his dreams, within reason. Not one who gave up on them entirely. I could do it all. Have a healthy balance of love, career, and family. And with Mac at my side, I could find it. I could have it all. Smiling, I closed my eyes, tightened my arms around her, and drifted off to sleep, feeling as if I were invincible…

And we were.

CHAPTER
Seventeen

Mackenzie

The next night I leaned against the wall, watching Austin perform on Captain Crow's stage from the backstage area. After spending the night in his arms, I knew more than ever that he loved me, and I would never doubt that again. A promise was a promise, and no matter how many fights we got in, or how many times I wondered if he wanted something more, I wouldn't let myself act the way I had before.

We'd talk. Watch our video. Love one another.

And most importantly, *never* give up.

He strummed his guitar; walking up to the mic with that sexy strut only he could pull off. On any other guy, it would look ridiculous. The crowd of girls went wild, and I smiled. I didn't blame them at all. I was going wild for him too. His biceps flexed as he strummed, his face intent as he sang the last note of his song.

As he finished, the crowd cheered, smiles on their faces as they yelled out how much they loved him. He grinned at the crowd, then turned and looked at me. I smiled and nodded, and his grin widened even more. Somewhere out in the crowd were Cassie and Quinn. I'd told them to come to the bar, and they'd been confused.

But they'd come…and they were about to see why.

Austin mouthed *I love you* to me, and I mouthed it back, my heart warming even more. How had I ever thought he didn't want me? Love me? Love like this didn't die.

It couldn't. We wouldn't let it.

He stepped up to the mic and leaned down. "So…I'm sure a lot of you have heard stories of me and Mackenzie Forbes breaking up."

The crowd stilled, nodding.

"Well, we did. And it sucked. It sucked enough that we realized…" He glanced over at me, and the crowd followed the line of his vision. He held his hand out to me, smiling. "We didn't want to be broken up anymore. And she's here with me tonight."

The crowd cheered, and I walked out, wearing my cowboy hat, my acoustic guitar, and a pink dress that hit right above my knees. Waving, I smiled at the crowd, walked right up to Austin, and kissed him in front of everyone.

Flashes erupted, and we both smiled against one another's lips.

"Was that romantic enough…?" he asked.

"And shit?" Grinning, I patted his cheek and stepped back. "Yep."

We settled into our stools, guitars in hand, and stared at each other. The last time we'd sung this came to mind, and the pain hit me all over again. We'd been so lost without one another. He reached out and squeezed my knee. The remembered pain was in his dark blue eyes, too, calling out to my own. But buried with that pain was hope and love. "Hey. It's me and you. Forever," he whispered in my ear.

LOSING Us

I nodded once, pressing my cheek against him for a second. "And always."

"I love you." Clearing his throat, his turned back to the crowd and raised his voice. "We're going to sing you our new song that will be on both our upcoming albums. We hope you like it as much as we do."

Settling into his stool, he nodded at me, and I started the chords that made up our song, "All In." As we sang, we locked onto each other the whole time, not looking away. It was a promise of sorts, as we sang to one another, ignoring the crowd. Ignoring everything but this…and *us*. Our vow to love one another and never let go again.

Never give up.

I didn't even notice until we finished, but tears streamed down my face again. This time it wasn't from pain or loss. It was from happiness, love, and hope. The second we finished, we sat there, breathing heavily, staring at one another. The crowd remained completely silent, no one moving, and I knew they'd experienced an intimate moment none of our other shows had ever felt. Or seen. They'd been here with us as we made vows. Vows that were more important than any other ones would be.

And I'd meant every word.

He swallowed so hard I saw his Adam's apple bob, and then opened his mouth, closed it, and said, "Marry me."

The collective crowd gasped.

Standing up, he set his guitar aside, knelt down on one knee at my feet, and held a ring out. He looked a little pale, and maybe a little green, but he'd never looked so beautiful to me. "Marry me, Mac. Be mine forever."

I tightened my grip on my guitar, unable to look away. Unable to talk, or move, because *this was it*. The one defining moment of my life where the answer would change everything. I knew what my answer was, obviously, but I also knew how big this was.

How *huge*.

His fingers twitched on the ring. "Mac?"

Tossing my guitar aside, I sank to the floor with him and nodded, throwing my arms around his neck. "Yes. So much yes."

The crowd erupted into cheers, and I heard Quinn's and Cassie's voices above them all. Cheering us on. Being happy for me. And I wanted to hug them so hard.

Austin kissed me, our tongues entwining. When he pulled back, tears swam in his eyes too. "Fuck, I love you, Mac. When we get home, I'm going to make love to you all night. Kiss every square inch of your body until you beg for mercy. And then I'll do it all over again."

He'd whispered it to me, so no one else heard it. Those words were just for me. My cheeks heated, and I leaned in close to his ear. "I'm all in," I whispered. "All freaking in."

He laughed and grabbed my hand, slipping the diamond ring onto my finger. "Rachel helped me pick it out today. I hope you like it."

"Like it?" I wiggled my finger, smiling as the diamond reflected the spotlight on us. "I fucking love it."

He tossed his head back and laughed, then stood and helped me to my feet. Hand in hand, we faced the crowd and bowed. After we straightened, I locked eyes with Quinn and Cassie, who whistled through their fingers and jumped up and down. I did a little dance in reply, and they cracked up.

Austin's fingers tightened on mine, and he tugged me backward. "Ready to make our exit?"

I nodded once. "Let's do it."

We bolted off the stage, laughing the whole way, not letting go of one another. As soon as we were backstage, he tossed me against the wall and kissed me, trapping me. Our lips melded, and he pressed his hips against mine, letting out a sexy growl. "Mine."

Nodding, I dug my fingers into his shoulders. "And mine."

Someone cleared his or her throat behind us, and I glanced over his shoulder. It was Rachel, Quinn, and Cassie. And they were all smiling as big as we were.

"Congratulations," Quinn said, rubbing her arms.

"Yes! I'm so happy for you!" Cassie said, coming up to us.

Hugs were exchanged, and then I made my way over to Rachel, who watched silently. "Thank you for helping your brother pick out the ring. I love it."

"I thought you would like the simple solitaire diamond." Rachel smiled and crossed her arms. She looked nervous. "You said as much in 'Take Me.'"

She referred to a song I'd written a few years ago on my sophomore album. "I did, didn't I?"

"Yeah..."

I hesitated, then pulled her aside. Austin watched us go, his brow furrowed, but he let us go alone. "Are you okay with this, Rach?"

"Yes, of course." She dropped her arms and shrugged. "I just...it hurt when you broke up with him and didn't talk to me at all about it. I thought we were family. That no matter what happened, you'd be there with me. With us."

I nodded, my heart twisting. "We are. And I'm sorry I did that. I just kind of...panicked, you know? I didn't think it through, but it won't happen again. I promise."

Rachel nodded. "Okay. Yeah. Sure."

"I love you, and I love your brother very much." I cupped her cheek and smiled. "I'm not used to being part of a family like this, to be honest. My dad died a few years ago, and I've been alone ever since. Until you guys. I'm still learning, too, but I promise to never make that mistake again. I swear it."

She relaxed a little, and a smile lit up her face. "Okay. I believe you."

I hugged her, and she hugged me back. She smelled like strawberries. So sweet and young. "Sisters forever?"

"Forever," Rachel said.

Austin came up, a soft smile on his lips. "Everything okay here?"

"Yes," I said.

"Perfect," Rachel said at the same time.

He grinned and threw his arm around both of us. "Time to go out and celebrate as a family. Where's it gonna be, kid?"

"Austin," Rachel said, rolling her eyes and punching him in the stomach playfully. "I told you to stop calling me that."

"It's my engagement night," he said, kissing her temple and meeting my eyes over her head. The love he had for her was so pure and strong. "Humor me."

"Okay..." Rachel met my eyes in silent communication. "In that case, let's go to Friendly's."

Austin laughed. "You want a cone head sundae, don't you?"

"So do I," I said quickly.

"Three cone head sundaes it is, then."

We walked out of the venue and cameras flashed. We smiled and posed for a second, then slid into Austin's Jetta. As we drove off, Rachel behind us in the backseat, we entwined hands, smiled at each other, and drove off into the sunset...

Together.

Quinn and James' Story Continues in

CHASING *Me*

It was supposed to be a love story....

I knew she was out of my league but I didn't care. Looking back, I wonder if I hadn't pursued her, would things have turned out differently? Is it Fate that determines our choices in life? God? Free will? Or just plain old innate selfishness?

I got her, of course. There hadn't been a girl I wasn't able to seduce. Problem was she seduced me right back, body, mind, and soul. She possessed me, tormented me, and showed me a world that was so bright and pure I was almost blinded.

Didn't she know after such a drug I could never settle for less? Didn't she realize no matter how many times I screwed up, or broke her heart, or bent her to my will, I'd never be able to let her go?

If I hadn't known such intensity existed, would it have been better for both of us?

True love, the real kind, isn't nice and sweet and pure. No, it's dirty, and sinful, and messy. It's like ripping a chunk of flesh from your body and watching yourself bleed out in slow, helpless intervals until you thankfully pass out.

This isn't a love story. But it's the only story I got.

Ty and Cassie's story continues in

FINDING *You*

Sex on the Beach, the do-over.

I had a simple plan for what to do in Key West the second time around.

Testify at the trial of the rapist I helped catch last year.

Make sure he gets locked away for the rest of his natural life, so he can never, ever hurt another girl.

Wait for my BFFs to get to town, so we can celebrate.

And stay far away from Ty Connor, because three months after breaking up with him, I still don't know whether being with him is worse than being without him.

Spring Break, take two.

All of the above? Out the window.

Turns out testifying is a lot harder than I thought it would be.

And not only is the rapist I helped catch not locked away, he's on the loose and looking for me.

Oh yeah, and it's definitely harder being without Ty than being with him, especially when I have to watch him with someone else.

Welcome to my world.